Kate and the Mystery Ponies

'Shasta. My lovely Shasta. She was really mine and I loved her.'

For Kate, it was like a wonderful dream. A horse of her own at last, and a chance to jump in the County Show. Then the suspicions crowded in. What was going on at the stables? She began to have doubts – was Shasta really hers after all? Was her dream about to become a nightmare?

A story for any girl who dreams of a pony of her own.

Sally Fielding

Kate and the
Mystery Ponies

A LION PAPERBACK
Oxford · Batavia · Sydney

Copyright © 1985 Sally Fielding

Published by
Lion Publishing plc
Sandy Lane West, Oxford, England
ISBN 0 85648 959 X
Albatross Books Pty Ltd
PO Box 320, Sutherland, NSW 2232, Australia
ISBN 0 86760 654 1

First edition 1985
Reprinted 1986, 1989, 1990

British Library Cataloguing in Publication Data

Fielding, Sally
  Kate and the mystery ponies.
  I. Title
  823'.914[J]   PZ7
  ISBN 0 85648 959 X

Printed and bound in Great Britain by
Cox and Wyman, Reading

Contents

1

How it all began . . .

IT WAS LATE JULY, the height of summer, and I was
kneeling on the soft lime-green carpet of my bedroom
leafing idly through old copies of *Pony*. Beyond the
clematis-framed window the sun stood unmoving
above the cornfields. Every leaf and flower glistened
with heat.

I was flipping through the pages, feeling really lazy.
Then suddenly an item on the 'Letters' page seemed to
jump out at me. For a few moments I knelt without
moving among the honeyed squares of sunlight, unable
to take it in. I read:

'Has anyone seen Roxy, my 14-hands crossbred Fell
mare? She disappeared from the field by our house
one night at the end of April. We think she must
have been stolen. She is a very pretty dark brown
with a white sock on her near fore and a narrow
white blaze. One of her top front teeth was broken.
'If anyone has seen her or can tell us anything
about her, please let me know. I miss her
dreadfully.'

The girl's name was Sarah Richardson and she lived
somewhere in Wales. In my sunny bedroom, the walls
covered with horse pictures, the pretty, printed flowers
of the duvet and curtains glowing in the light, I knelt
rigid as a statue, staring at the page. Two sentences
leapt out in perfect focus. *Dark brown with a white sock
and a narrow white blaze. One of her front teeth was
broken.*

I read the words again and again but my brain refused to accept them. All around me the house lay still and quiet. There was only me at home in the daytime. I turned to the cover of the magazine. Last month's. Then why hadn't I noticed the letter before? And if only I hadn't seen it now!

I got to my feet, stiff with kneeling, and sat at the little white dressing-table with the magazine still in my hands. But however often I read them, the words still said the same.

A small, framed photo stood at one side of the dressing-table. It was of me, my brother Chris, and Mum and Dad on the beach at Cromer. It was the last summer Mum was with us. Sea and sky were a hazy blue. Chris, tall and straw-haired, wore a striped tee-shirt and had just left school. Mum wore a yellow dress. I held a fishing-net and stood stiffly to attention, looking very pleased with myself. It was taken four years ago when I was ten. I gazed at it bleakly. How easy things had been in those far-off days, I thought!

At the opposite side of the dressing-table another photo showed a very pretty grey mare standing in a field by a fence. My lovely Shasta! And then I remembered the letter again and thought, Oh no! Why does life have to get so complicated?

I was jerked back into the present by the sudden loud tooting of a car horn. Not that time already! Dropping the magazine, I dashed to the window and saw Wendy's little red car waiting at the gate. Our gate stood side by side with our neighbours' gate, two houses in the middle of nowhere. I poked my head out of the window, called, 'Down in a tick!' and slammed it down. I tucked my shirt more firmly in my jeans, grabbed a comb and flew downstairs.

It was a Thursday, which meant that instead of slogging up to the stables on my bike I had a lift. I glanced quickly round the kitchen and living-room to check everything was switched off. It all looked neat and empty. Except for a used coffee mug on the mantlepiece it could have been a display in a shop. I grabbed the startled cat off the sofa and whisked her out of the front door, banging it shut behind us. She stood blinking on the warm brick step, rigid with disapproval, her black fur glistening. The youngest next-door girl, who had been playing with her mother's baking tins on their porch, now came and stood by the fence to watch us go.

Wendy leaned across to open the car door for me, saying, 'Sorry, Kate, I'm probably early.'

Wendy is like that. She always makes you feel at ease, as though nothing is ever your fault. 'You needn't have hurried,' she said. 'It's too hot to rush about.'

In her clean faded jeans and a sleeveless white blouse printed with forget-me-nots Wendy looked remarkably cool. Her arms were smoothly rounded and tanned to a lovely golden colour. Her fair hair was drawn back from her face and hung half-way down her back. The sunshine and the outdoor life that made me feel hot and red in the face had given Wendy a peachlike rose-and-gold look, and her grey eyes were clear and shining. Sitting beside her I felt all elbows and knees. My jeans were fraying a little and stained with hoof-oil. My arms were too thin; my stainless steel watch – passed on by Chris – too clumsy compared with Wendy's slender gold one. My hair needed cutting and the heavy fringe nearly hid my eyes.

It took about five minutes by car to reach Hollin Bank Riding School, where I worked before school and in the holidays. It was fifteen minutes at least by bike, and hard-going because it was all uphill. In Wendy's car we sped effortlessly past the cornfields, up the narrow twisting road through the woods and out among the sunny upland fields around the stables.

It seemed to me that the weather at Hollin Bank was always hot, as though the surrounding woods trapped the warmth and sheltered the tilted fields against the wind. The cart track branching off to the stables lay full in the sun. A few late foxgloves, glistening pink, shrunk against the hedge as if for shade. The stones were pale and chalky, the ground baked white.

I wondered whether to tell Wendy about the letter. But she had switched on the car radio and seemed busy with her own thoughts. She was twenty-two, a qualified riding teacher with three lots of pupils for lessons that afternoon and a new husband to get supper for. Sometimes the gap between fourteen and twenty-two can seem like a whole generation.

We swung through the propped-open gate into the stable yard, an oblong of cracked concrete with the dark bulk of the indoor school along the left-hand side. On the right and across the further end of the oblong were two rows of loose-boxes in an L-shape. Immediately to the left of the gate were the tack-room and feed-store and a small paddock.

Through a little gate a field-path led up into the wood. An opening at the further corner of the yard gave access to the jumping-field and the fields where the ponies lived.

Wendy pulled into the shade by the office, switched off the engine and reached over to the back seat for her hat. 'Half past seven,' she said. 'Okay?'

At the far side of the yard Mr Bryant who owns the stables was skipping out the boxes and putting down fresh straw for the night-beds. Rob, his son, was helping him. Wendy went across to join them.

Until last year, when I had come to work at the stables regularly, the job of riding instructor had seemed incredibly glamorous. Now I knew that wasn't the whole story. When she was not actually giving lessons Wendy worked as hard at the rougher jobs as the rest of us. Then, when her pupils were due to arrive, she tidied her hair and washed her face with cold water at the office sink, changed her jeans for jodhs and put on her good boots, so that she went out to meet them looking as fresh and neat as if she had just arrived.

But even so, it is still the job I would most like to do. Dad says that working with horses has no future, too many people and too few jobs, and that unless you are willing to work for peanuts you can forget it. The thing is that, in part, I know he is right. Which is why I pretend to go along with his idea of doing a secretarial course when I leave school. But privately I know I want to work with horses, whatever Dad says. I know it will take a lot of hard work and effort but I'm determined to get there.

I went into the tack-room, where it was cool and shady, and got Shasta's grooming kit from the shelf. In summer the tack-room door is left wide open, and the warm scents of outdoors mingle with the faint smell of saddle soap. I heard no sound, and jumped with surprise when I turned to find Rob Bryant standing just inside the door, watching me with a sort of superior grin. It was his most common expression and I hated it.

Rob was twenty-one. I knew this because the Bryants had had a party for him in the Easter holidays. The next day – a Tuesday, and luckily one of our quietest days – only Mrs Bryant's brother, Mr Betts who lived with them, had made it to the stables by six-thirty. He had been even more sour and silent than usual, which is saying something. Mr Bryant rolled up at about nine and Rob not at all.

Wendy and her husband had been at the party. But they hadn't invited me. Perhaps they thought I was too young. Chris, my brother, said, 'Well, after all you only *work* there,' and was surprised I had even thought

I might be asked.

Lucky Rob, I sometimes thought. *He* doesn't have to dream of a career with horses, it's all handed to him on a plate. He was a qualified instructor. He had done his professional exams at some expensive place in the Midlands where they kept top-class hunters that won prizes everywhere. He rode his father's horses at shows and, in a small way, was beginning to make a name for himself locally as a show-jumper with a big ugly chestnut called Coppernob.

Coppernob was more powerful, but in other respects he couldn't even begin to compare with my lovely Shasta.

Rob said, 'Dad wants you to take the five o'clock ride. The list is up on the board.'

'Right,' I said. I would give Shasta a work-out first in the indoor school. The hack would be a treat for her afterwards.

'Coming on nicely, isn't she?' Rob said in a conversational way.

I had to pass him on the way to the door. He fell into step beside me as I knew he would, and went on talking about Shasta. When Rob spoke of Shasta it made my flesh creep. She was mine — and I had paid for her. That phrase about 'the smile on the face of the tiger' always came to my mind.

Shasta saw us coming and whinnied and banged her door. I am sure she knew that when I came in the afternoon it was to take her out. But did she know, I often wondered, that she was actually *mine*? She lived all the time at Hollin Bank, was ridden by dozens of different people each week and was fed and cared for by whoever happened to be doing it that day. Did she realize, I wondered, that the tall thin girl who came slogging up each morning on a bike was different from the others, that by toiling up to Hollin Bank before school I paid for her keep?

One day I had ridden her down home to show her where I lived. I led her through the low gate and up the narrow path to the front door, thinking I would open the door and let her peep inside. But Shasta wasn't at all interested in the house. She just wanted to graze on the lawn and pull at the green chestnut leaves overhanging one corner.

I took her mints and apples and spoilt her rotten. Now in the holidays I groomed and rode her every day, dreaming of the exciting things we could do together.

I slipped inside the box, bolting the half-door behind me, and put down the grooming kit. Rob watched as I patted Shasta's grey neck and fed her mints from my palm. He said, 'I saw you taking her round the jumps yesterday. Getting ready for Tychwell I suppose.'

Tychwell was a small town about four miles away. I had entered Shasta for the Horse Show there.

'Will you be taking Coppernob?' I asked.

'Perhaps.' Rob implied that Tychwell Show was somewhat beneath him. He said, 'Now that you've entered for the County Show I suppose you need all the experience you can get.'

I didn't answer, but as I bent to pick out Shasta's hooves I was aware of his eyes always upon me, could sense his watchfulness as he leaned against the door. The sun edged his hair with gold, lit up one side of his suntanned healthy face and his blue shirt that matched the sky.

I don't like people watching me. It makes me nervous. I tried to ignore Rob.

He said, 'Well, if you want any help with her, just let me know,' and strolled away.

It was true. I did need help with Shasta. Not least, I needed a lot of advice.

When I had first dreamed of having a pony of my own I imagined myself hacking round the countryside on dewy summer mornings and romping around in gymkhanas. But dewy mornings found me up at Hollin Bank mucking out. And at sixteen hands Shasta was rather large for romping at gymkhanas.

At first it was enough simply to own her and ride her up at the school. Then, because she was so pretty, I began to think in a vague way of showing her.

It was Wendy who had noticed her talent as a jumper. Though I had been riding for two years I had never done much jumping. I had only tried tiny jumps in the indoor school and at first that was all I did with Shasta. But it soon became obvious – at least to Wendy – that Shasta was capable of far more. She put the jumps at three foot, four foot, four foot six, and still Shasta took them with ease. When spring came Wendy had suggested that I should consider entering her in competitions that summer.

'But do you think I'm good enough?' I asked, flattered but alarmed. So far I had never even ridden in a potato race.

Wendy laughed. 'Well, certainly Shasta is! I'd say she's done a lot of jumping at some time. And as for you – well, you've got to start somewhere.'

I would like to have started by having extra lessons, but lessons cost money and I was completely broke. Sometimes, when things were slack, Wendy or Mr Bryant (Rob was away at the time) had given me a session over the jumps. They taught me a lot, but I always felt embarrassed, feeling sure they must think I hadn't asked for extra lessons in the normal way because I was too mean to pay for them.

I dreaded letting Shasta down. Urged on by Wendy and financed by Dad I had registered her with the British Show Jumping Association, and – in a moment of madness – had entered her in the Foxhunter Preliminary competition at Hensingham County Show. Sometimes I woke up in the night and lay there panic-stricken, just thinking of it.

But when I needed help it would be Wendy I would ask. Not Rob.

At five o'clock I collected the children who were waiting in the yard and sorted them out onto ponies according to Mr Bryant's list. I suppose I must have seemed quite old to most of them; at least they were always quite respectful. I don't think they realized I wasn't a proper teacher like Rob and Wendy.

We filed out of the stable yard and through the little gate, onto the field-path which led up to the woods. The ponies were slow in the heat, flicking their tails and shaking their heads at the flies. Hooves clicked on stones in the dry earth. I halted Shasta by the gate, waiting to close it again, and said to the last girl through, 'Your reins are too slack, Helen. You're not making contact.'

Then suddenly, with a nasty jerk, I remembered the letter. Rainbow, the pony Helen was riding, was a dark brown crossbred Fell mare with a white sock and blaze and a broken front tooth.

2

Caught in the act

IT WASN'T ONLY THE COLOUR and the markings. I knew exactly when Rainbow had arrived at Hollin Bank.

It had been in the Easter holidays, when I worked afternoons as well as mornings. I had arrived one day to find Mr Bryant spreading straw in one of the empty loose-boxes. 'Is there another horse coming?' I had asked, quite excited at the prospect. 'What sort?'

Mr Bryant seemed to hesitate a moment. Then he said, 'Er, crossbred,' as if it was the first thing that came into his head. I thought it was because he was busy and didn't want to be bothered with me. But it had seemed odd for the owner of a new horse to be so offhand.

An hour later Rainbow had arrived – on the afternoon of Rob's birthday, 28 April.

Thinking about it now, I felt all churned up. When I got home I went up to my bedroom and looked at the magazine again. The letter was still there, the magazine was still last month's. How I wished I had never seen it!

But did I really think that Mr Bryant had stolen Rainbow? He might not have done it himself, of course. In fact, bringing her all the way from Wales would have been difficult. But had he bought her, knowing she was stolen? The markings and the broken tooth – especially the broken tooth – were powerful evidence. And she *had* arrived at the end of April. The fact that Wales was such a long way off meant that Hollin Bank would be a safe place to bring her.

As I thought about it all, it occurred to me that if Rainbow had been bought and paid for in the normal way there would be a record of it in the office files. In my mind's eye I could see the office at Hollin Bank. There was a tall grey metal cabinet with drawers, the lower ones stuffed to overflowing with magazines and show catalogues and leaflets about new veterinary products. Mr Bryant was always saying he must sort them out one day. He didn't like the office side of things and his method of dealing with paperwork was to throw it into a drawer and forget about it. But I knew that the top drawer of the cabinet was kept locked. Was that where he kept the account books? The more I thought about it, the more I longed to find out the truth about Rainbow.

When I went up to the stables and heard Mr Bryant

whistling cheerfully about the place as if he hadn't a care in the world and saw Rainbow grazing peacefully with the other ponies, I thought, 'It *can't* be true. She can't be the stolen Roxy.' Everything at Hollin Bank was too cheerful, too ordinary. Then I remembered Sarah Richardson, wondering if her poor pony had ended up on someone's dinner table.

I thought about it so much that I mentioned it to Chris, my brother. He snorted and said, 'You've got a good imagination, haven't you?' There's nothing like having a brother to put you in your place.

I put that particular copy of *Pony* right to the bottom of the pile and hoped I would forget about it.

Then something else happened.

It was the very next Monday, Mr Bryant's day off. Only Rob was at the stables when I arrived at eight o'clock. He was working over at the far side and I could hear his radio in one of the loose-boxes. When I found him he said cheerfully, 'Smashing day again. We're going to a sale over near Spenthorpe.'

'Anything special?' I asked.

'Nice five-year-old mare. Looks as if she might make a jumper. You can't tell until you see them. Still, it makes a nice day out.' He tossed an empty bucket across to me. 'I've watered as far as Gaylord,' he said.

I left Rob and the music behind and went to get on with my work. Stable buckets, in case you don't know, are half as big again as ordinary buckets and weigh a ton when filled with water. I staggered around with one in each hand and was glad of the cooler morning air. The sun shone full on the walls of the indoor school, casting a dark block of shadow on the concrete in front of the loose-boxes. Later the concrete would have to be swept. There was tack to clean and the feed-bins had to be filled. As the sun grew higher and hotter I thought with envy of the Bryants, setting off in the

Landrover through the shady woods. They would probably meet friends at the sale and have a leisurely lunch out somewhere.

But the hard work was worth it. For Shasta. I had had her since the previous autumn and I still couldn't quite believe my good fortune. A horse of my own had seemed so impossible. Sitting through the droning hours of maths at school or draped enviously on the rails at some horse show or gymkhana, I would dream of winning a pony in a competition, or of heroically rescuing a runaway horse from some dreadful fate (being run over by a train was the most usual one) and being presented with it by the grateful owner, who conveniently had no further use for it.

But life isn't like that. And in fact I got Shasta the most unromantic way you could think of — out of the redundancy money my father got when he lost his job.

Neither my father nor my brother was at all interested in horses, so I couldn't believe it when Dad said, 'Well, if you're ever going to get that pony, I suppose this is the time to do it. But you'll have to pay for its keep yourself. I'm not going to spend a fortune on it, but we'll get you a decent one.'

We didn't have far to look. I knew exactly the one I wanted — if only the price was right! Mr Bryant had recently acquired a beautiful grey mare, part Arab, six years old, sixteen hands, which he intended to bring on a bit then put up for sale. Every week when I went up for my lesson I would go over to her box and pat her hard grey neck and make a fuss of her, while she stood gazing straight ahead out of large long-lashed eyes, loving every minute of it. She would stretch her long neck over the door and gently nuzzle the pockets of my jacket to see what I had brought her.

Each week I'd go to Hollin Bank dreading to find the box empty and Shasta gone. Then the unbelievable happened, and on a wet and windy November morning

– the sort of morning that would never, ever, feature in rosy dreams – we drove up to the stables and beautiful Shasta was mine.

We had to pay much more than Dad expected. In fact, he looked thunderstruck when he heard the price, and there was tack to buy as well. But Shasta was worth every penny. Mr Bryant talked so much about her 'great potential' that I began to wonder why he wasn't keeping her himself. Then I realized that for a riding school you don't need 'great potential', only a sound constitution and a quiet temperament. He would sell her at a profit and buy something else.

I don't think Rob would have taken that view. Rob liked Shasta, he would have liked her for himself. But Rob was away on a course at the time. Now when he looked at her it sent shivers down my spine.

I kept her at Hollin Bank at half-livery. Shasta earned one half by being used for lessons and I earned the other half by working there before school, and at weekends and holidays. That just left me with vet's bills and the farrier. So far I'd been able to manage on pocket money and the extra money I earned by working in the holidays. But if Shasta had anything really expensive wrong with her I suppose I would have to pocket my pride and ask Dad or Chris, which is what they said would happen all along.

Soon after we got Shasta Dad went on a retraining course and used most of his remaining money on equipment and a second-hand van. Now he does electrical repairs, which seems to be working out quite well. I was glad about this. If he had hated it and wished he was back at the factory I would have felt guilty about having Shasta.

Chris thinks I am crazy, and there are times – such as that Monday morning with the yard like an oven and a mountain of tack to be cleaned – when I think he may be right. Cleaning tack is usually one of my favourite jobs but it gets a bit boring if there is no one to talk to. I wished I had brought my tranny like Rob. At eleven o'clock, with the yard outside dazzling with heat and an hour to wait before Wendy arrived, I got up and stretched and felt in my jeans' pocket for some money. In the office was a drinks machine.

The office had not yet been unlocked but there was a key in the tack-room. I went across and opened up.

The office is not very big and rather untidy. The drinks machine stands just inside the door and then there is a table with an electric kettle and some mugs. Opposite is a desk with a chair behind it. There are lots of photos and prize cards pinned to the walls and a notice-board covered with green cloth with posters and details of lessons and special feeds, written up by Rob or Mr Bryant.

I pressed the coins into the machine and collected my cold drink. As I stood in the office I found my eyes drawn to the tall metal cabinet in the corner. 'It's none of your business,' I told myself. 'It's probably all a mistake.' I fixed my eyes on the plastic cup of squash, the noticeboard, the yard outside the open door.

Except for the horses looking drowsily over their doors, the place was deserted. And I meant no harm. I only wanted to see one page, the end of April. Once I knew that Rainbow had been paid for. . . .

A cold shiver ran through me. What if she hadn't been paid for? What would I do then?

Gazing out at the cracked concrete of the yard, I tried to think back to that April day. A dark red horse-box . . . No, not a horse-box, a cattle-lorry. Rainbow had arrived in a dark red cattle-lorry with slatted sides. The driver was a boy in jeans and a black bomber jacket who hadn't stopped to chat or see Rainbow settled in but had unloaded and driven off at once, not even wanting anything signed.

Oh, this is silly! I thought. Chris was right — too much

imagination. *People like the Bryants don't have stolen horses.* Would someone with a flourishing riding school put it at risk for the sake of getting a pony on the cheap?

Then why not get it settled? said a voice inside my head. *There'll never be another chance like this. Or are you afraid of what you might find?*

If I looked in the drawer, who would know? In the noonday heat the place was quiet as a church. Blocking off that part of my mind that said 'no', I crossed to the desk and opened the right-hand drawer. The key was inside a tobacco tin. I took it out, small and flat and shiny, and fitted it in the locked cabinet. The drawer slid towards me, level with my chest.

I had never seen in this drawer before. Somehow, I had expected the stable accounts to be written in neat hardback ledgers with cash columns, like I had seen on sale at the newsagent's. Instead, there was just a jumble of papers and envelopes and well-thumbed notebooks. Some of the papers were held in bulldog clips; others had been put in loose. On the top, unfolded, was a typed letter from a bank, the heading printed bold across the top. Trying my best not to look, I moved it aside and picked up one of the notebooks beneath. The pages were blank. Oh heavens, I thought desperately, there must be *something!* Everybody had to keep records.

I picked up an old cheque book, empty except for stubs. Payments for feed, payments to the farrier. But there were no proper dates, only days and months recorded, not actual years. If only I could find one that said 28 April, with a large payment, large enough for a pony . . .

Quickly I hunted for other cheque books. The letter from the bank floated to the floor. Picking it up, I froze in horror. Someone was driving into the yard!

Swiftly I pushed the things back in the drawer, arranging them as nearly in the right places as I could.

As I shut the drawer a car door banged. Probably just a client, I told myself, my heart pounding. Probably someone to ask about lessons, who won't know that I shouldn't be here. . . .

Two steps took me to the desk. The key in the desk drawer. Footsteps close outside. I was still standing by the desk, flushed and guilty but without the key, when the tall angular shape of Mr Betts blocked the light.

My heart was thudding like a steam hammer, my lips were dry as sand. But my only hope was to look innocent. I lifted my drink to my mouth and tried to keep my hand from shaking.

'What's going on?' he demanded.

Mr Betts was Mrs Bryant's brother. He lived with them at the bungalow. He stepped inside the office, his flat bird-like head with its corduroy cap poking forward as his eyes skimmed the room. The skin of his highly-coloured face was stretched tight over the bones, giving him a gaunt appearance. The eyes beneath the tilted cap were hard and dark as pebbles.

'I came in for a drink,' I said, staring back at him. My voice came out high and strange.

'Behind the desk?'

On the wall at my back were cuttings from newspapers – Rob on Coppernob, Hollin Bank ponies at shows. I made a vague gesture. 'I like looking at the pictures,' I said in the same strangled voice.

I think he believed me, but against his better judgement. For a long time, the pebble eyes were fixed on my face, as though he could see into my mind. I realized with a sense of panic that if he had arrived a few seconds earlier he would have seen me at the drawer. Suddenly I felt quite weak and trembly. If Mr Betts knew what I had been up to I would be finished at the stables for good. And so would Shasta.

I said, 'I'd better get on,' and finished my drink while he watched me in silence. When I went round to the other side of the desk he moved ungraciously aside to let me pass. 'Just watch it,' he said.

I couldn't speak. With my face like a flame I marched across the yard. Back in the tack-room I flopped down on an old chair and sat trembling, staring at a row of saddles.

But I didn't see saddles. I saw a letter from the bank; a letter I would have given anything not to know about.

3

The mystery deepens

ALL MORNING I WAS ON PINS. Back home for lunch I cut my finger on the jagged lid of a tin and spilled some milk. Then I burned my spaghetti.

I was just mopping up the milk when Chris arrived home. He only did this now and again, and it always startled me because I was so used to having the place to myself.

He came into the kitchen, a lanky figure in blue overalls with very straight fair hair. 'What a mess,' he said, surveying the scene. 'What's the burnt offering for today?'

'Nothing that need concern you,' I said snappily. 'If you don't like it you can buzz off. I'd better get some sticking plaster.'

Chris unhooked a mug from the rack and made himself some coffee. 'What's the matter with you?' he asked. 'Fallen off the nag?'

'I haven't even been on her,' I said crossly. 'They've all gone to a sale.'

All except Mr Betts. It had never occurrred to me that he might not be with them.

'What it is to have money!' Chris said, settling down at the table with his coffee, and opening *Autosport*. 'All right for some!'

Chris was nineteen and an apprentice motor mechanic. Cars were his passion as horses were mine. He had an ageing Ford, which he called Doris, and he spent all his spare time messing about with it. His 'all right for some' remarks annoyed me intensely. He had far more money than I had. Besides, it wasn't all right for some . . .

'Chris,' I said, with a sudden urge to confide in somebody.

'Uh, yeh?'

What did I want to say? That I had been snooping in the office and seen something I shouldn't? If I didn't say what it was there would be no point mentioning it in the first place. And if I did say what it was I'd be making things worse, two people knowing instead of one.

'Oh, nothing.' I dumped myself on the bench opposite him, elbows on the smooth pine table, cradling my mug, looking fed up. I suppose I wanted him to notice and press me to say why.

Eyes glued to the magazine, Chris reached out for the bread I had put out for myself, folded a slice in half and put the whole lot in his mouth at once. 'Any cheese?' he asked when he was once more able to speak.

I decided to take the plunge.

'Chris, I'm worried about something at the stables.'

He didn't even look up. 'What's the matter? All the horses got housemaid's knee?'

'Oh, shut up,' I said.

Later, after he'd gone, I attacked the burnt pan with a wild desperation that had nothing to do with the baked-on contents. I couldn't have eaten it anyway. I couldn't have eaten a thing.

It was one of the afternoons I got a lift to the stables with Wendy. As I waited at the gate in the sunshine, the radio next door blaring out across the cornfields, I thought I would ask her in a casual way about some of the ponies, how long they had been there, where they came from. Wendy knew much more about Hollin Bank than I did.

But as we pulled away from the gate she said, 'I've been thinking about Tychwell Show. You ought to have a proper jacket.' She offered me an old one of hers that she thought would fit, and asked me about the classes I had entered. As it was all for my benefit, I felt I couldn't interrupt.

In fact, I had almost forgotten about Tychwell Show. I had been thinking about the much more important County Show at Hensingham two weeks later, and in the last few days I had been obsessed with my fears about Rainbow. I wasn't even sure that I wanted to compete at Tychwell, except that it would all be additional experience. I heard myself arranging to look at Wendy's jacket, and then we were at Hollin Bank and there was Mr Betts in his fawn shirt and cord trousers, red face under tilted cap, looking exactly as he had done when I'd left four hours ago. He glanced at me sharply but went on into the feed-store without speaking. The earlier encounter was still so vivid in my mind that I almost expected him to reopen our conversation.

I went for Shasta's grooming things. There was her dear familiar grey face looking over the door of her box. But I strapped her absent-mindedly, and the thought that in five days' time I'd be riding her at Tychwell Show had no reality.

Later on I decided to lunge her. Mr Betts had gone back to the bungalow. I wondered if the others were back yet from the sale.

Wendy had pupils in the indoor school so I led Shasta to the small paddock adjoining the yard, looped the lunge rein carefully round my hand as Wendy had shown me and started work.

I have read lots of articles by leading show-jumpers saying that lungeing is invaluable for keeping a horse supple and balanced. But Mr Bryant has no time for it, so as far as possible I try to do it when he's not around. Whether or not Rob shares this view I don't know. Probably not, though I've never actually seen him lungeing Coppernob.

Presently I heard voices in the yard. By the office door I saw Rob, hands in pockets, talking to his uncle and looking very pleased with himself. Mr Betts turned away and went towards the hay-loft. Rob came towards me.

Arms leaning on the fence, booted foot on the bottom rail, he stood watching me in silence. He looked like a cat with a saucer of cream.

'Had a good day?' I called, slowly circling.

The grin widened. 'Could say so!'

Beyond Rob in the stable yard I could see Mr Betts taking a hay-net to one of the empty boxes. Wendy's class came out of the school in little groups and trotted towards the pony field to unsaddle. Cars jolted down the cart track to collect them or bring others. Wendy trudged across to the office.

Rob seemed inclined to stay and I began to feel as if I was giving a demonstration. At any moment I expected some sarcastic comment such as, 'Where's the rest of the circus?' Rob made me uncomfortable more than anyone else I knew.

When I ignored him he called at last, 'Don't you want to know, then?'

'Know what?'

'If we bought the mare.'

I'd forgotten about the mare. I said, 'Well, did you?'

'I hate talking to somebody imitating a roundabout,' he complained.

'She's had enough anyway.' I gathered in the lunge

rein, noting with relief that Wendy was now coming across towards us.

'How did the sale go?' she called.

Rob turned to her. 'Pretty average.' But his smile said, pretty good.

'And what about the mare?'

The smile almost split his face.

'She'll be here in an hour,' he said.

I stopped, staring at him incredulously. 'You bought another horse?'

'Got it in one.'

I looked from Rob to Wendy, Wendy to Rob, feeling like every sort of idiot.

'Brown mare,' said Wendy. 'Rob's going to win the King George V Gold Cup on her.' She stood by him at the fence, the sun gleaming on her long, smooth hair and picking up the brightness of her watch as she rested her arm on the rail.

Rob laughed, looking pleased. 'There's a new pony for the school as well. Double Cherry.'

I turned away, glad that as I opened the gate they couldn't see my face.

'You don't seem very interested,' Rob said, addressing the back of my head.

'Of course I am.'

'Frightened she'll be better than Shasta?'

'If she's good enough to win the King George V Gold Cup she obviously is,' I said abruptly. Though I wasn't actually looking at them I was aware that Rob and Wendy were regarding me with surprise. 'I've got to go,' I said.

Leading Shasta back to her box, I remembered what we'd had to pay for her. The mare would have cost more than that, much more. And a pony as well! I felt almost sick. The words of the letter from the bank were spinning in my brain.

It was not a long letter. In a few seconds I had held

27

it I couldn't avoid seeing every word. It said that the bank could offer the Bryants no further credit, that unless they took immediate steps to put their affairs in order the bank would have to take drastic action.

In other words, the Bryants were broke.

There was something wrong. There was something terribly wrong. How could Mr Bryant buy new horses with a threat like that hanging over him? If the new horses had been for re-sale I could have understood it. He might make a useful profit. But Double Cherry was for the school and the mare was for Rob.

Then perhaps Rob was going to keep the mare and sell Coppernob? Or perhaps he had bought the mare himself?

I couldn't believe either of these. Rob clearly regarded the mare as his second horse, and I couldn't believe he had bought her himself. When it came to complaining about being hard up, Rob was almost as bad as Chris. Before he had bought his new jumping saddle he had sat in the tack-room for hours, working out his finances on the back of a cheque book, and asking my advice as to whether to get the saddle now and expensive leather boots later, or get the boots now and wait a while for the saddle.

No, the mare could only have been bought by Mr Bryant. And how could Mr Bryant afford it? I kept telling myself there must be some quite simple explanation. But I couldn't for the life of me think of one.

That day and the next were awful. I got snappier and snappier at home. I didn't even have much patience with Shasta. When one of the pupils at the stables broke a stirrup leather I nearly bit her head off.

At last, on the evening after the sale day, I blurted it out to Chris. He looked up from his magazine long enough to say, 'How do you know the bank came into it? He might have paid cash.' Which he seemed to think settled the matter.

'But the mare could have cost thousands of pounds,' I said wildly. 'He wouldn't have that much loose money!'

Unless he had sold other horses for cash. Horses that for some reason didn't appear in the account books. . . .

4

Sherry makes a discovery

FOR ALL MY SUSPICIONS AND FEARS, things at Hollin Bank went on as normal − pupils coming and going, the weekly visit from the farrier, preparations for Tychwell Show. One or two of Hollin Bank's pupils were taking their own ponies. But for the most part they weren't pony-owning sort of children. Mostly they came to Hollin Bank, as I had done, because it was cheap and if you hadn't got the proper riding clothes it didn't matter. You didn't even need a hat because you could borrow one from the office.

I suppose a lot of people would consider Hollin Bank very second rate, and think Mr Bryant rough and ready. But there must have been dozens of kids − perhaps hundreds by now − who would never have ridden at all but for the Bryants.

Sherry, who lived next door to us, was one of these. Their house and ours were joined together, standing by the road among fields. The mother, Mrs Bond, was fat and lazy, with frizzy permed hair and several chins. The three girls were given anything they wanted. They spent their time shrieking and pulling one another's dolls' hair out and letting their pet rabbits out onto the road. In summer with the windows open we heard everything that went on.

Mr Bond, small and energetic, was a part-time fireman, part-time gardener, part-time rat catcher, part-time night watchman and on Saturdays put up and took down the stalls for Tychwell market. In the afternoons he watched golf and racing on telly with his feet on the sofa and a can of beer in his hand.

When he stopped me by their gate one day and said that Sherry, the eldest, wanted riding lessons, I thought it would be just a passing craze and expected her soon to give up. But Sherry had got quite keen and we cycled up together on Wednesday afternoons, Sherry on Chris's bike. After lunch there would be a rising crescendo of yells, shrieks and threats as Sherry was got ready. Then a clatter of the gate, a single loud bang on our front door, and Sherry would be standing on the step with her greasy hair slicked over to one side, holding a biscuit between her teeth while she struggled with the zip of her jeans.

As we left home on this warm Thursday in July we could hear the younger girls demanding to go swimming.

A light breeze swayed the leaves and made dancing shadows on the road. High clouds drifted in a sky of infinite blue. After the easy run between the cornfields we got off and plodded up the hill, into the airy shade of the woods. Though she was only ten, Sherry was tough as old boots. She never got left behind.

Like the rest of her family, she thought that because I helped with the beginners sometimes I must be awfully good.

'Rob's got a new horse,' I said as we freewheeled the last little bit into the yard.

It was a few days after Rob's bombshell, and I had had time to think. I had thought of something that I ought to have realized before. Though I couldn't help seeing the words of the letter, I hadn't noticed the date. The letter could be months old, years perhaps. Probably the bank account had been put in credit ages ago, which was why Mr Bryant could now afford new horses.

This thought had come to me while cleaning my teeth after lunch, and was like a great weight rolling off my mind. Why hadn't I thought of it earlier? As I parked my bike and heard Mr Bryant whistling in the feed-store I felt like whistling too. What an idiot I had been to get worked up about it!

Sherry buzzed off for her lesson and I went to see to Shasta. After collecting her grooming kit I went swinging across the yard in a blissful state of perfect happiness, thinking how lucky I was to be up at Hollin Bank on this glorious day with a horse to ride.

When I got to her loose-box Shasta wasn't there. For a split second I stared at the trodden straw, the dangling hay-net. Then panic hit me. Where was she? She was *always* there! She gave rides in the mornings, and at week-ends she was used by the school all day. But she had always been there in the afternoons. Always!

I ran to the feed-store to find Mr Bryant, but Mr Bryant had gone. I dashed across to Wendy with her little group of mounted pupils. Shasta was not there. 'Where's Shasta?' I gasped.

Wendy looked vague. 'I think I saw Rob with her,' she said. 'Try the small field.'

I ran round the side of the indoor school to the field. Rob was going over the jumps on Shasta, watched by his father.

It came as a shock, because Rob had never ridden Shasta before without asking me. Or had he? As I stopped and watched it came to me that in the long hours I was at home or at school, Rob − or indeed anyone else − could do what they liked with Shasta, and I'd never know a thing about it. The thought was

31

horrible, as though Shasta wasn't really mine.

As long as he doesn't lame her, I thought wildly. Or overtax her. Or overface her with jumps too large, so that she loses her nerve. . . .

It was hateful to see Rob in charge of Shasta. I thought that when I appeared he would stop and bring her across to me; but he went on, and the jumps were too high. He was riding full tilt like he rode Coppernob, pushing Shasta on where she would have held back, stick always at the ready. 'Can I have her now?' I asked. The question sounded abrupt and much louder than I intended it to be.

Mr Bryant turned to me. His cheerful face expressed surprise.

'I want Shasta,' I said.

Mr Bryant called to Rob. Rob took Shasta over the next fence with a whack of his stick, then turned and trotted towards us.

'I don't like you doing that,' I said, my face burning.

Rob swung lightly from the saddle. Standing there with the two men I suddenly felt very insecure, very much alone. Their cheerful faces, so alike, looked down at me with identical grins.

'You want to keep her going,' Rob said, handing me the reins.

I didn't know what to say. Shasta was sweating, but not too much.

'He does know what he's talking about,' said Mr Bryant.

'It's just that I want to train her in my own way.' It sounded petty and ungracious after all Mr Bryant had done for me. 'I'm sorry,' I said. 'I know she has to be ridden for lessons but I'd rather you didn't jump her.'

'I suppose you'd rather some ham-fisted pupil had a go.'

I felt miserable. Rob had ridden all his life and was a qualified instructor. I ought to have welcomed his advice. And Mr and Mrs Bryant had always been so kind to me.

With an attempt to sound light-hearted I said, 'It's just that if she's going to go lame I'd rather do it myself!'

I meant it jokingly, to relieve the tension, but it sounded as if I thought Rob would lame my horse and I felt more miserable still.

Sherry stayed on after her lesson. When the five o'clock lot had ridden out of the yard with Wendy and I'd tacked up Snowstorm and Ben for two girls who were coming for a lesson with Rob, Sherry and I set to work on the evening watering − sixteen horses living in, thirty-two big buckets. I said to Sherry, 'We'll get all the buckets collected up to start with.'

We began at the end near the gate with Grenadier, the big grey. He is seventeen hands and towered above Sherry, the biggest horse in the stables. When you're in his box he has a habit of laying back his ears and swishing his tail and shifting his weight from one back foot to the other as if he is going to kick. It can be quite frightening until you get to know him. He is really a big softie. Sherry had a couple of fruit sweets in her pocket and when she held them out on her palm he bent his long neck to take them, snaffling with his lips. When he had finished, he shook his head and bared his yellow teeth. 'That's his way of asking for more,' I told her.

Next to Grenadier was Betty, Mr Bryant's oldest horse. She is very spoilt and loves to be made a fuss of. When it is nearly feed time she is always the first to start whinnying and banging her door. If you feed any of the other horses first she makes a dreadful racket.

Prince next door was out with Wendy. Next to Prince was Caprice, one of the two horses at Hollin Bank at full livery. He belonged to a very smart middle-aged lady who absolutely worshipped him. He had fantastic tack and a rug with his name on, and no one else ever rode him. When I went in for his buckets he knocked the remaining water all over the floor and my feet.

The other full livery was next to Caprice, a dun called Hollyhock who belonged to a girl called Susi something. I had never discovered Susi's other name and always thought of her as Susi Hollyhock. In fact I once called her that to her face. Actually I think Hollyhock is a silly name for a horse, though as he is rather a long-legged creature it seems to suit him quite well. Susi is as slim as a post and taller than me even though she is younger.

Beyond Hollyhock were three empty boxes – Seth out with Wendy, Snowstorm and Ben out with Rob. Next was Shasta with her head poking over the door to see what I was doing. After Shasta were Clancy, Posy, Jewel and Jade, all out, then Peppermint, Coppernob, Rob's new brown mare, Fandango, and Bluebell. The last box had its door shut and was not in use.

When the buckets were collected by the tap we started filling them, which is the most boring thing ever. Sherry asked, 'Which one is Rob's new show-jumper?'

I pointed out Fandango and Sherry went across to stroke her nose. I moved the heavy bucket from under the tap and, when two were filled, left the tap gushing into the third while I staggered across to Grenadier with the first two.

Sherry came back. 'Can I have a go on Shasta afterwards?' she asked.

'I suppose so.' I was thinking that when we had finished I would put Shasta over the jumps and Sherry could pick up any I knocked down (which sounds mean but she wasn't exactly being a great help with the watering). Then I would let Sherry have a few turns round the yard. When I thought of jumps, I remembered that Shasta had already had a session that afternoon with Rob, and my stomach gave a little lurch as I thought of the way he had whacked her and urged her on. How could I hope to train her to my own style unless I had her to myself? She was no longer mine to do what I wanted with, to school with my own methods. Rob drove her on. Rob used his stick. Rob could ride Shasta more or less whenever he wanted to.

I thought bitterly, if I do badly at Tychwell I'll know who to blame!

I heard an engine and looked up to see Mr Bryant driving into the yard in the Landrover. The Bryants rarely walked to the stables, even though their roadside bungalow was only a field away. There was very little garden at the bungalow. To one side was a concrete area where the Landrover, trailer, Citroen (Rob's) and horse-box were parked. To be honest, I think the outside looked a mess – too much concrete and a manicured rosebed. But inside it was very lush and modern, with lovely carpets everywhere and a kitchen like an advertisement.

Mr Bryant drew up by the tack-room. Then the Landrover door shot open and he leapt out.

'Get away from there! Get off!' he yelled.

I looked at him in amazement. But he wasn't shouting at me. He was hurrying towards Sherry, who stood, looking guilty, by the closed door of the empty loose-box. 'Leave it alone!' he shouted.

I was astounded. What on earth had she been doing? I know that some people dislike the Bonds, but surely Sherry had been doing nothing wrong?

'She's helping me,' I said.

'Oh yes?' Now that Sherry had rejoined me by the tap Mr Bryant had calmed down. His crinkly face was rosy from working all day in the sun.

'There's a horse in there,' Sherry announced. 'It's all shut up.'

I think Mr Bryant reddened, but it was difficult to say. He said, 'That's right.'

I thought it must be the one they got at the sale, Double Cherry. 'I'd better get him some water,' I said.

'No, no, leave it. He's very nervous. Needs time to settle.'

'But –'

'I said leave it!'

I had been going to say, 'But why is the top door kept closed?' Why keep Double Cherry in the dark? But though I was puzzled I wasn't going to argue. Thirty-two buckets were quite enough for me.

The telephone rang in the office. After a last doubtful glance at Sherry, Mr Bryant went to answer it. He came out with a piece of paper in his hand and went towards the indoor school.

'I want to see the pony,' Sherry said stubbornly.

'You heard what Mr Bryant said. He needs time to settle down.'

'*Settle*!' Sherry's voice was pure scorn. 'He's quiet as a corpse.'

She was right. I had been at Hollin Bank most of the day and never even guessed he was there. I had assumed that when Double Cherry arrived he would be put in the field with the other ponies. All the ponies lived out. So why was Double Cherry in a box?

I thought that he might be ill and said to Sherry, 'Perhaps he isn't well.'

Then why had no one been in to see him? And why was I not even allowed in with water? What were they afraid I might see?

My imagination's running away with me again, I thought. Anyway, it would be easy enough to check. If he was ill, there would be special feeding instructions on the office notice-board.

Sherry was taking Hollyhock's buckets. 'Back in a minute,' I called to her.

I went into the office and got myself a drink. I needed to cool down after all that hard slog. While I drank it, I glanced through the notices on the board. A note for the farrier – Peppermint near fore, Jewel hinds, Coppernob full set. Lists of lessons. A scrap of paper saying, 'Check hay Thurs.' Nothing about Double Cherry. Oh well, I thought, he's probably not actually ill, just nervous, like Mr Bryant said.

I sauntered out into the sunshine holding my cup of orange. Where was Sherry? She wasn't in the yard. Along the little path from the wood I could see Wendy returning from a ride with a group of children, a slow procession of colour against the green. By the gate our bikes winked in the sun.

And then I heard a bang, and there was Sherry swiftly shooting the bolt of the end loose-box.

'What have you been doing?' I said sharply, feeling responsible.

'Having a look.' Sherry's eyes sparkled. She was not at all ashamed.

'You were told not to go in there!'

Sherry practically danced across the yard, a girl with an exciting secret. 'Yes, and I know why!' she said.

She held up a hand, fingers spread, before my face. The ends of the fingers were dark brown.

'But what is it?' I asked, mystified.

'Dye!' she announced triumphantly. 'The pony in there has been dyed!'

5

An unexpected visit

SHERRY WIPED THE STAINED FINGERS down her jeans, dark brown streaks on the blue. 'I'm dry as a lemon,' she declared.

Glad to take her mind off Double Cherry I gave her some money for the drinks machine. Children were arriving with their parents in cars for the six o'clock ride. The children in Wendy's class were dismounting. Sherry drained her drink in about two seconds, tipping the cup high in the air, while a group of chattering girls came towards the office.

'Let's get Shasta,' I said, anxious to get Sherry away from everyone.

We did some jumping but my heart wasn't in it. *Why do people dye horses?* I kept asking myself. And the only reasons I could think of were ones I couldn't accept.

Sherry had her turn on Shasta then we gave her a rub down and a feed and set off for home.

Whizzing down the hill with the rush of air in our faces and the gravel flying from under our wheels Sherry yelled, 'Why did they do it, do you think? It wasn't all over, just where the saddle would be, where there might be a freeze-brand. Do you think Mr Bryant is a crook?'

'Of course not,' I said, staring straight ahead at the road. 'The trouble with you is, you've got too much imagination!'

The next day was Thursday. Just a week since I'd seen Sarah Richardson's letter. When I rattled into the yard in the early morning sunshine my eyes went straight to the end box. It was firmly shut. From the other boxes horses' heads – grey, chestnut, black or bay – poked in inquisitive rows. But the end door was just an oblong of green paint.

As I parked my bike I saw Mr Betts going towards it with a hay-net. He let himself in through the end door, shutting it behind him. My heart seemed to miss a beat. What would he say if he knew that Sherry also had been behind that forbidden door?

If only I knew what to do! The only person I could think of who might have explanations – I mean the only person I felt able to ask – was Wendy. Perhaps I could ask her that afternoon as we drove up to Hollin Bank?

But in fact I saw Wendy sooner than expected. I got back home from the stables at about ten and had just sat down in the kitchen with a great pile of toast, some coffee and a book when the door-bell rang. I wondered whether to ignore it, sure it must be either Sherry or someone selling something.

However when the bell rang again I got up and peeped out of the kitchen window. Wendy's red car was at the gate, so I hastily swallowed what I was eating and dashed to the door.

I was surprised to see Wendy at that time of day. She had never been to the house before except to collect me.

'Come in!' I said. 'Would you like some coffee?'

She stepped in out of the sunshine, looking very summery and pretty in a pink skirt and a sleeveless white blouse. She was carrying a large brown paper bag. I hadn't tidied the living-room but it looked all right because we had a family rule that everyone must put away their own things. The only thing lying about was my own sweater on the sofa.

Wendy handed me the bag. 'I think it should fit,' she said 'It's just a bit too tight for me. The jacket,' she added, seeing my blank expression.

I took the folded black jacket out of the bag and held it up by the shoulders. When Wendy had said 'my old jacket' I had thought she meant 'old' as in 'decrepit'. But this was just like new!

'Try it on,' she said.

I slid my arms into the jacket, straightened the collar, fastened the buttons.

'Fits a treat,' said Wendy, turning me round to see the back. 'It's wool so I'm afraid it has to be dry-cleaned, but it's a good make.'

I held my arms out sideways, pretending to admire the cut and the fit. The embarrassing moment was upon me.

'How much do you want for it?' I asked, trying to sound casual.

Wendy looked surprised. 'I'm not *selling* it. It's a present.'

'But – well, if you advertized it in the paper . . . ' I blushed and floundered.

'All right, then. If you insist on payment I'll have that cup of coffee.'

I can't tell you how relieved I was! I'd been worrying about how to pay for the jacket ever since she had mentioned it. I'd even been hoping it wouldn't fit. 'But are you sure? I mean . . .'

'Absolutely,' she said as she followed me into the kitchen.

I moved the dirty plate to the draining-board and busied myself with getting Wendy's coffee. She sat on one of the benches.

'Second breakfast,' I explained, moving the pile of now-cold toast. 'I always come back starving.'

There is something very cosy and friendly about kitchens. I wondered if it might be a good time to ask about Rainbow and Double Cherry.

'What a nice room,' she said, glancing round at the sunny apricot walls, the pine units, the pretty tiles.

'Yes. Dad did it himself.' It *was* a nice kitchen, though I was sure Wendy's own must be nicer. Her husband is a doctor and they have a big house just outside Tychwell with a gravel drive and lots of lilac trees. 'Have a biscuit,' I said, wondering how to lead into the subject of stolen ponies.

Wendy took a shortbread from the tin and I sat down opposite her. As always, she looked a knockout. Her skin was peachy gold against the crisp white blouse. Little golden tendrils escaped from her tied-back hair.

She looked happy and relaxed.

The house was totally peaceful. I would never get a better opportunity. I could tell her all about my suspicions in complete privacy. It would be such a relief. No one but Wendy would know.

No one but Wendy . . . Wendy, who had known the Bryants for years; Wendy, so open and friendly and uncomplicated, who would never even dream of such things herself . . . And what would she think of *me*, I suddenly wondered, if she knew what nasty thoughts lurked in my mind?

I played about with my spoon and said, 'I'm really thrilled about the jacket. I'd thought I might perhaps get one for Christmas or my next birthday. It's really fantastic.' I paused, then said in a rush, 'Wendy, there's something I've been wanting to ask you about. I mean at the stables.' Wendy's clear grey eyes gazed across at me enquiringly. I felt small and mean and unworthy and the words died in my throat. 'What I mean is – well, perhaps you've noticed I've been all churned up . . .'

Wendy looked across at me sympathetically. 'That's because you're worried about the show on Saturday. Everyone gets like that at times, especially when you're not used to it. I'm hoping to be there myself. Is Rob taking Shasta in the box?'

So the moment passed, and nothing was said.

When Wendy had gone I went upstairs and flopped onto my bed, despising myself for not taking the chance while I had it. In three more hours I would be leaving again for the stables. Nothing seemed less attractive. Why on earth did this Rainbow business have to come along and spoil my summer?

The day was warm and sultry. A midday stillness hushed the fields. Even the Bond household was quiet, as though subdued by the prospect of the afternoon heat.

I lay on my back with my hands behind my head, trying to shut out the worries of the morning and the duties of the afternoon. On the wall opposite was my poster of two ponies, a grey and a chestnut, standing by a hawthorn tree with buttercups at their feet and a cloudless blue sky overhead. Printed across the buttercups were the words, 'God is Faithful'.

Mum had bought me the poster when I was ten and it is still one of my favourite things. The poster probably had something to do with the time I first wanted a pony. The two in the picture are really beautiful. I wasn't too sure about the 'God is Faithful' bit. At least, sometimes I was sure. When we had bought it my mother had pointed to the words and said, 'Remember that, Kate.' Now it was too late to ask her what it meant.

Today, however, even the lovely ponies failed to cheer me. I said out loud, 'Oh God, if you *are* faithful, please help me!' The house seemed very still and empty. Perhaps I ought to go to church more, I thought. We'd got out of the way of going very much, with housework and stablework to do on Sundays. I seemed to be getting out of touch. Life was all school and work and Shasta.

I gazed at the two lovely ponies, friends for ever under a sky of infinite blue. If only I had a friend of my own, I thought longingly. A girl that I could have fun with and share the things that were important to me. My best friend at school lived six miles away, and had other friends where she lived. We hardly ever met in the holidays. I couldn't just ring her out of the blue and start nattering on about Rainbow! And then a thought came into my mind — if God *is* faithful like it says perhaps he would send me a friend if I asked him?

I know you can talk to God anywhere, but it never seems quite right to be too casual about it. I got off the bed and knelt down, hands together and eyes closed as I had done since I was little. I knelt there in the perfect silence and held in my mind the amazing fact that the Lord of all the universe is also my heavenly Father, who loves me and wants to give me the things which are good for me. Then I felt a bit ashamed, because I was only remembering to talk to him – I mean really talk, not just say a pattern of words – because I wanted something.

I said, 'Dear Father, I'm sorry I let things crowd you out of my life. I always go my own way, and forget about your way, then wonder why things go wrong. I thank you that you love me. Please, God, I need a friend. Please lead me to the *right* friend: And somehow bring it all about.'

It occurred to me when I had finished this prayer that the friend might turn out to be someone I already knew, but had failed to pay enough attention to. Or it could be someone completely new. It was quite an exciting thought that God himself was now taking charge of this for me. As I got to my feet, I marvelled that I'd never thought of turning it over to him and asking for his help before!

I wondered who the person would be? A girl of about my own age would be best, I thought. And interested in horses. And preferably a nice sympathetic sort of person with a sense of humour as well. But now my thoughts had drifted and it had begun to sound not so much like a prayer as an advertisement for a penpal.

It says somewhere in the Bible that God knows our needs even before we ask him. It's just that he doesn't come barging into our lives until he's invited. Now I had asked him, and I was sure that he already knew just the right person. I ran downstairs two at a time, feeling more light-hearted than I had for days. I heated frankfurters and baked beans for my lunch and realized with surprise that I was actually singing.

Afterwards I tried on the jacket again, turning this way

and that to admire the effect in the mirror. And I thought with surprise, Yes, God *does* know what we need before we ask for it, because this morning — before I had even prayed for a friend — Wendy (who had never come into our house before) had arrived quite out of the blue with the jacket and to reassure me about Tychwell Show.

I suppose it could be called a coincidence, but it seemed to me like a promise. Not that Wendy was to be the friend, but that God already knew my need. Wendy's visit was a sort of first instalment to assure me that in due course the rest would follow.

How would it all work out, I wondered?

6

Tychwell Show

THAT AFTERNOON AND THE NEXT DAY, Friday, whizzed by at lightning speed. There was so much to do for the show.

Rob had decided to take Fandango and had offered me and Shasta a lift in the lorry.

'But if Fandango is as good as Rob says, she must be well above Tychwell's standard!' I said to Wendy. 'They'll win every class. The other competitors will lynch him!'

Wendy said, 'He wants to see how she reacts to crowds. She's quite highly strung, I think.'

During that week Wendy and I tidied Shasta's mane and tail, which Shasta hated. Rob lovingly polished his new saddle and mixed extra supplement in Fandango's feed. No one else in the yard had entered.

It was to be a busy week-end at Hollin Bank. Apart

from the show, a group of children were coming for a riding holiday. The Bryants run four of these holiday weeks each summer. Each week sixteen children come to stay, sleeping in tents in the little field next to the bungalow. The Bryant's kitchen looks like a bomb site all week and Mrs Bryant makes great panfuls of food which she dishes up on trestle tables under the trees. As well as learning to ride, the visitors are supposed to learn stable management. In theory, this means that they do our work for us, but it's not such a doddle as it sounds. A lot of them just come to lark around and you have to watch them every minute. Last year some of them got up at crack of dawn and were discovered chalking their names on the roof of the indoor school.

Sherry thinks the camping weeks are great, regarding them as an open invitation to spend her days at Hollin Bank, and strutting about taking the visitors on guided tours of the horses and generally giving the impression that she owns the place.

Saturday morning seemed to arrive so quickly that I didn't have time to be nervous. I had to be at Hollin Bank by half past six. It was a beautiful morning, clear and bright. When I passed the field Mr Bryant still had not put the tents up. The bungalow door stood open to the early sun. Cases of Coke were stacked by the step.

Mr Betts, Mr Bryant and Rob were already at the stables. Rob had led Fandango into the yard. How calm and elegant she looked! He had washed her the day before and put on Show Sheen. Now in the sun she shone like rich brown satin. Rob was adjusting her plaits.

'Going to be a scorcher,' he said as I passed. 'We want to leave at nine-thirty if you can make it. Mum said come up to the house for some breakfast.'

'I've brought some bacon sandwiches.'

'Save them for your lunch.'

Before starting to muck out my four boxes I went to Shasta. She stood waiting, her ears pricked, and greeted me with a whinny. Did she sense that today was The Day, I wondered? I had been telling her about the show all week.

Shasta moved from foot to foot, her ears alert. 'Yes, we'll soon be setting off,' I said, patting her long grey neck. 'Your very first show. You'll like it, Shasta.' As I spoke I realized that I didn't know if it *was* Shasta's first show. In fact, it was most unlikely. 'Anyway, it's mine,' I said.

Perhaps it was as well I had so much to do before leaving. Otherwise I would have been shaking like a jelly. My normal morning's work was to muck out Shasta, Clancy, Snowstorm and Ben after the Bryants had fed them, then do their hay-nets. This morning I had only got as far as Snowstorm when Mr Bryant came and said, 'OK. Leave it now. I'll finish off.'

'Oh thanks,' I said, handing over my fork.

'Nervous?' Mr Bryant's crinkly blue eyes looked at me kindly.

'I will be when I get there.'

I led Shasta into the yard, hosed her down and got busy with the water brush. That's the trouble with greys. However clean they are the day before, there are sure to be some stable stains by morning. I had washed her tail the previous evening and plaited it all the way down like Wendy showed me, to keep it clean. All I had to do with it this morning was to unplait.

All the same, I had to be quick. Everything took more time than I had imagined. I was trying to do things carefully but my fingers were clumsy. It was after nine by the time I had put on her travelling bandages and tailguard and cycled up to the bungalow. Rob had left the yard ages ago. I found him in the kitchen, already washed and changed, shirt crisply white, tie neatly knotted, cream jodhs immaculate and boots gleaming with polish. He was eating eggs and bacon.

'Yours is keeping warm in the grill,' he said, pointing with his fork. 'You'd better eat it first and get changed afterwards.'

I had brought up my things in a carrier bag. After gobbling my breakfast I went into the bathroom to change.

I always find other people's bathrooms fascinating – a glimpse into the family's private life. This one had thick warm dry towels in dusty pink; cream tiles on which dark red dolphins sported; a dark red bath and a really enormous mirror over the basin. But I had little time to admire it for while I was still doing my tie Rob's voice called, 'Are you ready? We should be off.'

I shoved my jacket and hat back in the carrier on top of my work clothes and went out into the little hall. Through the open door I could see the lorry waiting at the gate. Mrs Bryant came out of the kitchen with an apron over her jeans and a towel in her hands. 'Good luck,' she said. 'Don't worry if you don't do too well. Everyone has to start somewhere.'

'Thanks – and thanks for the breakfast.'

'That's all right. You'd better go, they're waiting.'

Mr Bryant and Mr Betts had loaded the horses down in the yard. Now Mr Betts sat high up at the wheel of the horse-box with the engine running, his fingers tapping impatiently. Rob was next to him. I climbed in next to Rob. As I banged the door after me the lorry was already jolting forward up the lane.

'Is Shasta all right?' I asked.

'Seems happy enough.' Mr Betts was a man of few words. He concentrated on the road and kept glancing at his watch.

'Sorry if I kept you waiting,' I said.

We soon covered the five miles to the show-field. In the two main rings the early events were already in progress. Horse-boxes and trailers were ranked solid along one side of the field with more arriving all the time. We had to park at the far end and were lucky to find a place where the tall hedge behind gave some shade. We jumped down from the cab and Rob went at once to put in his late entries and collect our numbers. Mr Betts and I let down the ramp. We led out Shasta and Fandango and tied them up in the shade with their hay-nets and water. 'Hold the fort for a minute, will you?' said Mr Betts. Then he too disappeared.

There were lots of people about. Everyone was either busy or going somewhere. I patted Shasta's neck, wondering what she made of it all. I saw nobody at all that I knew. Above the roofs of parked cars I could see the bobbing heads of competitors as they cantered round the ring.

The morning's events in Ring One, away to my right, began with classes for young stock and ponies in hand. The bobbing heads were in Ring Two, where the Junior Jumping for ponies of 13.2 and under was in progress. Rob and I had both entered the Local Jumping which followed this, and also the Open Jumping later in the day.

When Rob came back he was grinning cheerfully and accompanied by a girl of about twenty. She had red hair looped back into a net and wore jodhs and wellies and carried a riding stick.

'Jolly nice nag,' she said, standing back to admire Fandango.

'Not bad, is she?' Rob stood with his arms folded and spoke with satisfaction. 'I'm hoping for great things. We've got some good horses in at the moment.'

'Yes, what about this other one? *Most* impressive? Where do you manage to find them all?' They were looking now at Shasta.

'That one's mine.' It came out more forcibly than I had intended and I felt myself blushing.

'Well, lucky for you,' said the girl, giving Shasta a friendly slap.

Rob turned to rummage in the cab where we had stowed our stuff. 'Anyone want coffee?' he asked.

'Good idea!' the girl said enthusiastically. She turned and grinned at me enquiringly, unsure of where I fitted into the picture but willing to be friends nevertheless.

'Not for me. I think I'll just look around for a bit,' I said, feeling uncertain.

'You've got twenty minutes at least,' she said.

It was glorious on the show-field that bright August morning. The sun, already high overhead, sparkled down on the rows of parked vehicles, the patient queue at the ice-cream van, the spectators clustered at the rails. Through the gate at the far end a slow procession of lorries, cars and trailers was still arriving, while neat little children in hacking jackets bobbed proudly about on ponies. And everywhere you looked there were horses – some waiting, some competing, some warming up for their events.

I squeezed through to the rail. A girl on a little bay mare was going round the 13.2 course. They thundered along past me on the other side of the rails, knocked down a gate and swung round towards a brush fence.

Suddenly my stomach was in knots. The girl galloped out as the loudspeaker announced the number of faults. Heads turned to watch as the next competitor trotted in. Within the hour that would be me! I looked at the large oblong of grass, the ribbon of people all around the rails. Even the jumps for the 13.2 looked big and solid. 'I must have been crazy!' I thought. I was almost sick.

'Six more to jump,' announced the loudspeaker.

I squeezed out again. Time to put in Shasta's studs before walking the course. In fact more than time! I had come further from the lorry than I thought and for a few panicky minutes I could not see it at all. All the lorries that had arrived later were parked beyond us so that we were now towards the middle of the line. When at last

I found it people were applauding the winners of the last class.

'Sorry I'm late!' I panted. Rob was saddling Fandango. 'I've got to do Shasta's studs. I haven't picked out her feet –'

'Calm down,' Rob said. 'She's all ready.'

'But –'

'Feet, hoof-oil, studs. All you have to do is saddle up. I'll even ride her for you if you like. Anyway, there's no great panic, they've still got to alter the fences. Have some coffee while you wait. They'll give it out on the loudspeaker when it's time to walk the course.'

I had forgotten that the course had to be altered. I drank the coffee and felt calmer. Then I fetched Shasta's saddle and bridle from the lorry.

Rob said, 'I meant what I said about riding her for you. She could do well with the right handling.'

'I'd rather ride her myself,' I said, wishing that Wendy was there to bolster me up.

Rob shrugged. 'As you like. When is your turn, by the way? I'm glad I'm near the end. I like to see what the competition is.'

'I didn't think of going to look,' I said, sure it must make me look totally thick. 'I'm getting really scared.'

Rob grinned. 'Join the club,' he said.

'*You're* not scared. Not with the great Fandango!'

'Jealousy will get you nowhere,' Rob said easily.

Close to, the jumps looked massive and even more solid. The parallel looked especially daunting – two poles like young tree trunks supported in deep metal cups. I tried to imagine Shasta taking me over them. Instead, I could only see her catching a foot against one of the those heavy unbudging poles and the two of us being flung head first to the ground. Rob inspected the poles without comment and started pacing out the distance to next fence. I strode beside him, trying to look capable and experienced.

The girl with red hair joined us and flashed us her wide toothy smile. 'Don't look so scared,' she said to me. 'It's a jolly nice course. Much better than the stinker they'll give us later for the Open!'

Though this event was limited to riders living within a ten-mile radius of Tychwell, there must have been more than twenty people walking the course. Afterwards, when I went to look at the blackboard in the collecting ring, I found there were twenty-four, of which Rob was to jump twentieth. My own name came third. The red-haired girl was apparently called Sue Kettlewell and was number seventeen.

'Well, at least you won't have to hang around getting into a twist,' Rob said to me. 'You'd better go and get Shasta.'

'I wish I had gone over the practice jump first,' I said nervously.

'I shouldn't let it worry you,' said Rob.

As I rode Shasta down to the collecting ring I felt quite light-headed and strange. There were lots of riders there already, and they all seemed to know one another. I gave my name to the steward and waited quietly by the entrance, stroking Shasta's neck and hoping to look as if I was on my own by choice. Rob and Sue were talking to some friends nearby. The first competitor trotted into the ring.

The course had looked horrendous but they had no problems going round it, and came out with a clear round. The next competitor, a girl on a big chestnut, trotted in as she came out. The mare reminded me very much of Coppernob, powerful but graceless, and with the same bright colour. They had three fences down including, I noticed with relief, the second pole of the parallel which had seemed so frighteningly solid. They thudded out past me to a smatter of applause. Then, my heart racing madly, I heard the loudspeaker announce 'Miss Kate Leigh on Shasta' and rode forward into the ring.

It was like a nightmare. We stood for what seemed like hours while the men replaced the jumps. I have never felt so conspicuous in my life. Shasta twitched her ears and seemed restless. I patted her while a thousand eyes watched. To calm myself, I went over the course in my mind — straight down one side, across the far side, back across the middle then swing right towards the brush fence — quite a sharp turn there. . . .

Suddenly the bell rang. I pressed Shasta into a canter and we were off. At the first fence, an oxer, the pole thudded down behind us. The next fence was on us almost instantly. Somehow we were over it and round the corner to the double. Then the gate. For a hideous moment I thought I had gone wrong and had to pull sharply round. We hit the dreaded parallel with a great clunk and the whole lot crashed down behind us. 'Steady now, steady,' I muttered as Shasta's rhythmic hoofs thudded towards the next jump. But it was myself I was talking to, not Shasta.

As we turned towards the brush fence I thought I glimpsed Wendy at the rails. Perhaps that was what calmed me, or maybe the realization that more than half the jumps were now behind us. For suddenly I was aware that all that lay between me and the finish were four fairly straightforward jumps, that the sky was blue and the air sparkling. And here I was, competing on my own lovely horse at a proper show!

Shasta took the last four jumps like a bird and I rode out feeling on top of the world.

Back at the lorry, I found Mr Betts sitting in the cab with the windows open, reading a newspaper and smoking a cigarette. He glanced up as I swung down from the saddle.

'Six faults,' he said. 'I should think you're quite pleased, aren't you?'

I gazed at him in amazement. 'I was awful!'

Mr Betts turned over the newspaper, looking unconcerned. 'It said six faults on the loudspeaker.'

'I suppose you're right.' Now I came to think of it — though it had seemed a real mess at the time — I had only knocked down two fences.

'Not bad for a beginner,' he said.

I unsaddled, gave Shasta a brief rub down and put on her fly-sheet. 'You darling lovely horse,' I said, stroking her nose as she nuzzled sugar from my hand. I left her in the shade with hay-net and water while I went back to see the rest of the class. The loudspeaker was announcing the fourth clear round.

I met Rob on his way to fetch Fandango. 'Well done!' he said.

'It was terrible!'

'You should push her on more. Use your stick.'

'It wasn't that.'

He strode on towards the lorry.

'Good luck!' I called after him.

I found myself a little space by the rail next to a family with two children and a dog. In the ring a man on a roan was demolishing every jump in sight. At least I hadn't done that!

By the time Sue Kettlewell went into the ring on a cobby-looking mare there were six clear rounds. Sue's was the seventh, Rob's the eighth and last.

Fandango was a very neat jumper and fast on the turn. I felt unexpectedly proud to see Rob being awarded the red rosette. Fandango stood tall and elegant, her brown flanks and neck bright as satin.

'Won that easy,' said the man next to me.

'Yes, she's tipped to win the King George V Gold Cup,' I told him. I really think he believed me.

The hours until my next class seemed endless. The programme, as usual, was running late. I ate my lunch early then wandered round the field. But, although I had plenty of time, I couldn't relax. I hoped I might see Wendy, or someone I knew. But I saw no one. When I returned to the lorry I found only Mr Betts, dozing in the driver's seat with his cap tilted over his eyes.

Everyone seemed to be either with someone or looking for someone. I adopted an air of purpose, telling myself I was looking for Rob or Wendy. But when I did come across Rob − swigging something from a can in the refreshment tent with a crowd of men − I slipped away again unnoticed.

If only I had somebody to talk to! Even Sherry would be better than no one. I remembered my prayer for a friend. Perhaps I might even find her here − today? After all, what better place to find a horsy friend than at a horse show? But all the girls I saw seemed to be either with other girls or with their families. If Mum was still alive, she would have come with me for sure.

I thought of Mum, happily humming to herself as she went about her chores, and the words of the song 'What a friend we have in Jesus' floated into my mind. I thought about Jesus. He had experienced far greater loneliness than mine while he was on earth. 'Dear Lord,' I thought, 'please help me. You know what it's like.' As soon as I said this I realized how pathetically self-pitying it sounded, as if I expected every little part of my life to be smooth and easy. And as I looked around me, I found myself saying, 'Thank you for bringing me here with my own horse on this lovely day. Thank you, because you're going to find me a friend. And help me to be a good friend.' It wasn't at all what I had meant to say.

At this point, for no apparent reason, I thought of Chris, who was probably alone at home tinkering with Doris. I could have asked Chris to come. He might even have enjoyed it. I would certainly ask Chris to come to Hensingham. We could watch the other rounds together. I would tell him how nervous I was, and we could have a picnic lunch from the back of the car like a proper family.

Perhaps it was the thought of the big County Show at Hensingham that banished my nerves at Tychwell. Hensingham put Tychwell in perspective. Before my next appearance in the ring I had a few turns at the practice jump and then won myself a rosette in the Clear Round jumping in Ring Three. I thought to myself, 'Well, even if I *am* on my own, I'm still enjoying it!'

The course for the Open Jumping was much more difficult than that for the Local. As I walked it all my fears came flooding back. 'Use your stick,' Rob advised me when we met in the collecting ring. 'If you push her on you could well be in the money.'

It was a big class. I did try to push Shasta on a little, like Rob said, and felt that my six faults was quite a creditable result. Once again Rob was in the jump-off and once again an easy winner.

'I told you you'd sweep the board,' Mr Betts said to him as we loaded the horses. 'That horse has class.' After the Open, Rob and Sue had gone on to win the Pairs Relay.

'You've got class, too,' I whispered to Shasta, stroking her neck. But I couldn't quite keep out the uncomfortable thought: with a better rider might she also have had some prizes?

Jolting out of the show-field in the cab, I suddenly realized how tired I was. It had been a good day but now I could scarcely keep my eyes open. And we still had evening stables to do.

The traffic was slow and Rob and his uncle were silent. My thoughts went to Hollin Bank where the holiday-makers would be chasing rats in the feed-store and concocting apple-pie beds. And then my eyes closed.

7

The ET's settle in

IN FACT I SAW VERY LITTLE of the visitors after we arrived
back at the stables that evening. They are usually
known in the yard as the ET's − which doesn't stand
for what you might think but is short for *enfants
terribles*. This is what Mrs Gale who owns Caprice
always calls them, ever since one of the earliest groups
(so it is said) decided to try the horses out on chewing-
gum. 'Now, don't let the *enfants terribles* feed Caprice
with anything unsuitable, will you?' she says anxiously
to Mr Bryant. 'Do make sure the *enfants terribles* don't
use Caprice's tack or bucket.' She is some sort of high-
up secretary and rarely visits the stables except at
week-ends. Then she wears very smart riding clothes
with real leather gloves and her hair in a net and rides
Caprice at shows.

Of course the ET's themselves, knowing nothing of
this, are happy in their ignorance and assume we all
think of them as lovable extra-terrestrials.

Though most of the work had already been done by
the Bryants I was dead tired by the time we finished
evening stables. As I cycled back up the track from the
stables to the road, wearily pushing the pedals, I met two
girls and a boy whooping merrily along in the opposite
direction. The boy had a babyish pink face and a cap
like Mr Betts'. The girls, who were about twelve, wore
bright purple lipstick.

'Keep going!' yelled the taller girl as they raced past.
'They're gaining on you!'

'Take yer brakes off!' advised the boy at the top of his
voice.

If those three are typical, I thought, heaven help us.

Passing the bungalow, which stands where the track joins the road, I noticed Chris's bike propped by the wall. Evidently Sherry was also having fun.

When I got home I found both Chris and Dad in the kitchen. Chris, lolling in his usual corner seat at the table, was reading a mag. Dad was loading the washing-machine.

'How did you get on?' Dad asked.

'Not too badly. At least it wasn't too bad when I'd stopped being nervous.'

'You won then?' said Chris.

'Ha, ha,' I said, slightly sarcastic. Why are brothers so annoying?

Dad said, 'If you get changed now your things can go straight into the washer. I thought we'd just have scrambled eggs for supper.'

'So jump to it with the eggs, girl,' said Chris, seeing that I lingered by the sink.

'I'm whacked. How about *you* doing it for a change?'

'Who do you think did the shopping?' Chris said, turning over the pages of his magazine.

I suppose it was fair enough, especially as I would be out again for most of the next day. But it made me realize that to expect Dad and Chris to come to shows with me was not very realistic.

I went up to change and got the supper together. As we ate our scrambled eggs followed by apple pie with cream, I told them about my day – the crowds and the excitement and Rob winning on Fandango. As I relived the day, I realized that it had been really good. Much better, no doubt, than Chris's time spent working on Doris or Dad's long hours indoors re-wiring a workshop.

I said, 'I'll be out again most of tomorrow. I've got to help with the ET's. Take them for a ride or something.'

'They forecast rain,' Chris said kindly.

The rain came late that night and was heavy. It was strange to wake up next morning without the familiar sunshine on the curtains. The world outside was veiled and damp. At half past six I ate my breakfast alone in the kitchen, listening to some bird chirruping in the bushes. Just before seven, when I pushed my bike out through the little front gate, the misted air had a luminous look. Big drops of rain hung on the fence.

The long climb up to Hollin Bank brought me out into sunshine. Even the most shabby parts of the stables had a washed and sparkling look.

The ET's breakfasted at eight but most of them were already at the stables when I arrived. A small group of them, including the boy with the ratting cap, were being shown by Mr Betts how to fill hay-nets. Mrs Gale's Range Rover and trailer were parked in the yard.

The horses whinnied and banged their doors, impatient for food.

'All right, all right,' I said, as Grenadier, the big grey whose box is nearest the place where I park my bike, neighed imperiously. 'I'm coming as fast as I can!'

There is a special atmosphere about the yard at week-ends. It is extra busy as the people with horses at livery usually come up. Often they are getting ready to go to a show. There is a lot of dashing about from box to tack-room, agonized shouts of 'Who's whipped my dandy brush? What on earth did you do with his rug?', until at last the horses are loaded, the doors slammed, and the lorries and trailers depart slowly up the track. In no time at all, it seems, the first people are arriving for their lessons and we are working flat out all day. Then we notice, almost with surprise, that the day is cooler, the tired competitors are already returning, and that the present lot of pupils is the last.

Today Mrs Gale and Susi Hollyhock were going to a hunter trial, sharing Mrs Gale's trailer rather than taking their separate ones. They were loading their horses when I arrived. Mrs Gale was fussing about some miniscule variation in Caprice's plaits and telling Mr Bryant to be sure to have a feed ready on their return. Caprice is certainly a nice horse, but from the way she goes on you would think he was the only thoroughbred in existence.

Susi came into the tack-room. She is the fair and willowy sort of girl. She looked like an advert for riding clothes.

'You look smart,' I said.

'Thanks. You haven't by any chance been using my grooming kit?'

'No, I've got my own.'

'It's just that the leather-dressing has gone.'

'Oh, I'm sorry. Would you like some of mine?'

'It's a bit late now. We're ready to start. Anyway I got some from Rob.'

'I'll have a look for it,' I promised. 'It couldn't be the ET's. Well – I mean, they've only just arrived. And it's not the sort of thing they'd want.'

A horn tooted outside. Mrs Gale was ready to start.

'Well, keep an eye on the little horrors,' she said. 'Last time they were here they swiped my bucket.'

She dashed out into the yard and across to the Range Rover. The hunter trial was some distance away and Mrs Gale liked to leave in lots of time. For a moment I felt a stab of envy. How I would have loved to be going with them – driving off in an almost-new Range Rover, everything smart and well-organized and no horses to see to but my own? Somehow theirs was a different world.

Rob was also off to a show, though not until later. It was a bigger affair than Tychwell. He had entered the Grade C jumping, scheduled for mid-afternoon. But Rob's world was more like my own. We both had a morning's work to do. In fact, to be honest, Rob always worked hardest of anyone.

'It would be nice if you could make it four wins in a row,' I said, as he stood waiting for his first pupils to saddle up.

'Oh, there'll be some real class horses there,' said Rob, full of confidence nevertheless. 'If you had pushed Shasta on a bit, you'd have been in the money yesterday yourself. You've got to show a horse who's boss.'

'That's not my way,' I said, defensive again.

'You'll learn! With the right handling that horse could be a winner. When we get to Hensingham I'll give her a warm-up for you.'

'Don't get her going *too* well. She might beat Coppernob,' I said, teasing him.

Rob laughed. 'I won't worry about *that*!' he said.

It was a beautiful morning for riding, warm and hazy with a pleasant freshness in the air. In the shadows of walls, still untouched by sun, the grass was wet and the dark earth soft and moist. I wondered if there had been rain at the shows where our horses were going. Muddy jumps were something I had never tried.

The ET's were in the pony-field where Mr Bryant was choosing ponies for them. They usually stick to the same pony all week, learning to groom and care for it. Of course, the ones who have been before head straight for the ponies they know will do well and win lots of rosettes in the final gymkhana on Friday. (I'm not criticizing them for this. In fact, if winning is important to you it's the sensible thing to do.) The rest generally want a particular pony because they like its looks.

Mr Bryant asks them how experienced they are, eyes them up for size, and fixes them up with suitable mounts. The two girls I had met in the lane had grabbed our two skewbalds.

Two of the biggest children were arguing over

Bellboy, a liver chestnut, very showy-looking (and a complete slug, though they didn't know it.) My own favourite among the ponies, a little Welsh mare called Snowdrop, had been given to a red-haired girl with freckles. Snowdrop is a real sweetie. When you go to put on her head-collar she pokes her nose down into it to help you, and though she's only 12.2 she'll have a go at anything. The freckled girl looked sweet too. Paul, the boy who had told me to take my brakes off, was standing with Rainbow.

At the sight of Rainbow I was stricken with guilt. Here was I, enjoying myself at shows, working all day at a job I loved, my own horse safe and cared for, while poor Sarah Richardson moped at home with nothing to ride and wondered all the time if her poor Roxy was now tins of cat food. I had scarcely thought of it for days.

But what could I actually *do*? I asked myself for the hundredth time.

I glanced round the field for an unfamiliar pony that could be the new Double Cherry, a dark brown pony like the dye on Sherry's hand. Surely he couldn't still be closed up in the loose-box? Yet he was certainly not in the field.

All sixteen were now fixed up. Three of them were complete beginners and would have to be shown absolutely everything. They had been given the oldest, quietest ponies. In fact, all our ponies are fairly quiet because any that aren't are sold on. The possible exception is Danny. Danny can be a real pig. If he doesn't want to canter he will buck instead; if he doesn't want to jump he'll either stand rooted to the spot or shoot off like a rocket. Visitors always admire Dan because of his striking appearance and the showy way he prances about. But he's certainly not a novice ride.

Today he had been claimed by a tall girl called Lara – probably the oldest in the group. She had bold grey eyes, a wide pouting mouth, and wore a white Costa Brava tee-shirt with gaudy palm trees and a donkey wearing a sombrero.

'Did Mr Bryant say it was OK for you to have Danny?' I asked as we led the ponies down to the yard.

'Why not?' Lara gave me a challenging stare.

'It's just that he needs an experienced rider.'

'You don't say!'

We tied the ponies in the yard, and as I saw one of the others helping her with her quick-release knot I realized that our conversation had told me precisely nothing. I should have persisted, or asked direct as Wendy would have done. I always make a mess of these things.

The ET's crowded round me and I began my bit. 'This morning I'm going to show you how to groom a stabled horse,' I said. 'From now on your ponies will be kept inside, in the row of boxes round the back, and you'll be responsible for looking after them. I'm going to show you the whole routine, though you won't need to do it all each day.'

After checking their knots I led them in a straggling bunch to the tack-room to show them where everything was kept. 'And don't touch anything else,' I warned them. 'All those things on the top shelf belong to people who have horses at livery here. By the way, I don't suppose any of you know anything about a missing bottle of leather-dressing, do you?'

Thirty-two round eyes gazed back at me, the picture of utter innocence. Leather-dressing? they seemed to say. *Leather*-dressing? Whatever would we want with leather-dressing?

I fixed them up with an assortment of brushes, curry-combs and buckets — anything that was spare really — and set them to work.

Luckily for me, most of them had done some grooming already. Stuart often helped his older sister with her horse and was both sensible and experienced. I learned that Rainbow's rider, Paul, had been on these camping holidays twice before, and that the conscientious little girl with Snowdrop was called Clare.

The only boys on the course, besides Paul and Stuart, were two brothers called John and James Digsby-something who had 'come to see what it was all about' but seemed to spend most of their spare time at home sailing. They also played cricket, tennis and squash, and last week had come first and second in an orienteering competition. They were bright, well-mannered boys, eager to please and to do well. But if something was not up to standard, I sensed, they would not be slow to say so!

The purple-lipstick girls, Sandra and Tracey, were at the end of the line and continually overcome by giggles. Whenever I went over to them, they would straighten their faces and try to be hard at work, only to collapse in giggles again the moment I had gone.

We finished just before one o'clock, when Mr Bryant came to inspect their work. Then, tired and thirsty, we made our way back up the track to the bungalow. The sight of large jugs of lemonade and packed lunches laid out on the tables in boxes was greeted with delight. There was a great scramble for seats and paper cups and soon everyone was enjoying their egg sandwiches, tomato sandwiches, portions of pork pie, chocolate biscuits, crisps and apples.

It was cool and pleasant in the field as the tables were in the shade of three big apple trees. The air was still fresh from the rain. Though I call it a field, I suppose it's really the Bryants' back garden, because the bungalow opens directly onto it and Mrs Bryant hangs her washing there. The grass is bumpy and unkempt, not at all as Dad would have it. Apart from the ultra-neat doll's-house garden at the front, the Bryants don't seem to have much time for gardening.

When we had almost finished, Rob came out of the back door. All heads turned to watch as he sauntered across the grass towards us. His creamy jodhs, shining boots and crisp white shirt were met with stares of admiration, and for some reason he was already wearing his red jacket. He came and stood casually, hands in pockets, next to where I sat at the end of the table and glanced down at the muddle of cups, wrappers and boxes that now littered the bare boards.

'Any lemonade going?' he asked.

I pointed at the nearest jug and Sandra quickly pushed a clean cup towards him. In a leisurely way, watched by rows of eyes, Rob poured himself a drink.

'What do you think the going will be like?' I asked.

'A bit soft, perhaps. Difficult to say. There hasn't been as much rain there. I phoned to ask.' His blue eyes narrowed as he glanced up at the sky. 'Anyway, it soon begins to dry out with the sun on it. Yesterday the ground was a bit too hard for my liking.'

'Are you riding at a show?' one of the little girls asked timidly.

Rob gave her an indulgent smile and I said, 'He's got a very good show-jumper called Coppernob that wins lots of prizes. He's a Grade C, which means that he's registered to take part in big competitions. It's only Coppernob's first season, though,' I added quickly, seeing the Digsby-whatsits disapprove of Coppernob's Grade C status.

'It's still not *very* good,' replied James. He and his brother wore jaunty white baseball caps with red peaks and the name of a sports car across the front, which seemed to set them apart from, and somehow above, their merely horsy neighbours.

By this time Paul was impatient to say something. He did not like being left out of the conversation. 'You ought to do something about all the fleas or whatever they are. They were all over us last night. I couldn't 'enjoy my supper,' he said rather loudly to Rob.

There was a sort of awed hush.

'You mean the midges,' I said, hoping to goodness he did.

'Something like that. They fly around and bite you. This garden is full of them.'

There was a murmur of agreement.

'When we go camping,' James told Rob, 'we buy these special things that you burn to keep them away. You get them from camping shops.'

'Oh, wrap up!' Lara told him rudely. 'It's not Rob's fault!'

Rob said nothing. He looked at his watch. I said, 'I suppose you'll have to be leaving.'

'Time waits for no man,' Rob observed with a sigh. He grinned briefly at the rows of upturned faces. 'Enjoy your ride!' He turned and went, quickening his pace as he neared the house and bounding lightly up the kitchen steps.

'Good luck!' called Lara, watching him every step of the way.

After this encounter with a Real Live Showjumper we turned to the more mundane task of clearing up the mess on the tables. Dregs of lemonade were tipped on the grass, cores and crisp bags and wrappers were stuffed into an empty box to be thrown away. I sent Tracey for a cloth to wipe the table.

'This afternoon I will take the more experienced ones for a hack,' I told them. 'The others will have a lesson in the paddock with Mr Bryant. There'll be two other girls who come for a ride every Sunday afternoon joining us. I think we'll go through the woods.'

We went down to the yard to saddle up. I felt on top of the world because they were impressed when they knew that Shasta was my own. She looked so tall and calm and aloof among the little ponies. The two local girls who were joining us arrived and went into the office to pay and to find out which ponies they were to ride.

The sun was warm. The sky was a cloudless cornflower blue and the woods looked fresh and inviting. No one wanted to stay behind at the stables and ride round the paddock!

Mr Bryant had given me a list with the two groups of names. Among groans and protests I sorted out the ones who were to stay. The beginners' group was made up of the younger girls, as well as John and James. They trooped slowly off into the paddock where Mr Bryant was waiting.

I glanced round my own group, all mounted and eager to start. 'Are we ready to go?' I asked.

They all nodded.

'Everything checked?'

More nods. Then Snowdrop's rider went pink and dismounted. She said, 'We didn't check their feet.'

'Speak for yourself,' said Lara. She and her friend Annabel stayed loftily in the saddle, but all the others got off and started to check their ponies' shoes for loose or missing nails.

When everyone was mounted again we set off through the little gate and onto the field-path which led to the woods. The children filed ahead while I fastened the gate and followed behind on Shasta. It was a wonderful day. Everything sparkled. It was glorious to be out in the fresh green countryside, to feel Shasta's eager stride and the warm air against my face. Butterflies flitted across the grass and the trees stood heavy with leaf in the full beauty of summer.

Then I noticed that Lara and two other girls were well ahead and already entering the wood. I pressed Shasta forward to catch them up. This was no time for feeling poetic. With the ET's around you couldn't relax for a moment!

8

Adventure in the wood

I CAUGHT UP WITH CLARE and three of the younger ones as the track entered the leafy shade of the wood. It was not a dense wood. Splashes of sunlight patterned the ground and the wide brown bridle path was still damp and soft in places from the rain. I could see Lara and the others ahead of us.

After a short way the path divided. Lara and her friend were waiting for us, impatient to go on. 'Which way?' they called as we approached.

I didn't answer but waited until we had caught up with them. Then I pointed to the path on the right which led on up the hill. They set off at a brisk pace and Stuart and Paul pressed on after them. 'Don't get too far in front!' I called.

Sandra and Tracey, still giggling and muttering to one another in secret were lagging behind. I beckoned them to hurry then went on after the others. Really, the ET's were a menace at times!

Clare on Snowdrop was telling me about the pony she rode at home. She had a riding lesson each week with her sisters, who were at present at Pony Club camp. She was a sweet little kid with round grey eyes and an earnest expression. On the other side of me rode Emma on Bobby. Karen, one of our regular pupils, usually rode Bobby on Sundays but now she rode a weird-looking appaloosa called Measles (which wasn't his proper name but referred to his spotty appearance). Measles had a thin neck and a large ugly coffin-shaped head. He hated work at the best of times and Karen kept up an endless stream of complaints about him to her friend Caroline, who fell into the mood of things by grumbling non-stop about her pony Starshine.

'I think Mr Bryant ought to give us extra time, riding these things,' grumbled Karen. 'An hour's hardly long enough even to get them out of the yard!'

Caroline on Starshine was not to be outdone. 'This one's a real bone-bag,' she said. 'He must be eighty if he's a day.'

'You ought to be glad you've come here riding at all,' I told them, feeling very like a school-marm. 'Lots of girls would give their eye-teeth to be up here in the woods on a pony.'

'They wouldn't give their eye-teeth if they knew they'd be riding Measles,' said Karen, digging her heels into his spotty white stomach in an attempt to urge him on. 'For sheer excitement you might as well sit on a sack of hay for an hour!'

I said, 'He's like a mule. You'll never get him to move by pounding him with your heels. Look, Lara and the others are out of sight again! Come on, Measles,' I said, going alongside and clicking at him encouragingly. 'Perhaps if the rest of us canter on he'll try to keep up with us.'

We set off at a canter up the woodland track. Glancing over my shoulder I saw with relief that Measles was cantering along behind.

I was anxious about the four who had gone on in front. We should all have kept together. Goodness knows where Lara and Co. might be by now! But after a couple of minutes we rounded a bend and found them sauntering just ahead, laughing and joking.

'Please keep with the rest of us,' I said as we caught up. 'If you don't I'll have to tell Mr Bryant and he might keep you back at the stables next time.'

Lara gave me an unfriendly stare. She was the oldest of the group, probably only a year or so younger than me, and she clearly didn't like being ordered around. 'Oh dear, who's teacher's pet then?' she said, with a sneer.

'If you're as experienced as you say, you should *know* that you don't go rushing ahead,' I said, feeling flushed and put out. As I said it, I realized that Lara hadn't said she was experienced at all – at least, not to me. In fact, she had carefully avoided saying so. But Mr Bryant must have been satisfied or he would never have let her have a pony as zany as Dan.

At that moment Sandra and Tracey caught up. 'Please try to keep with the rest of us,' I said. 'We'll all enjoy the ride so much more.' I knew it was coming out wrong – I sounded like a prim old teacher with a difficult class.

Sandra and Tracey caught each other's eye and giggled. Clearly they were enjoying the ride very much as it was.

The path, winding gradually upwards, now dipped into a wide hollow where the trees were older and more spaced out. Stretches of bracken grew among the great gnarled roots. In spring there are sheets of yellow celandines and the path winds among clumps of violets. Beyond the hollow we usually continue on a path going gently down the long shoulder of the hill. The upward path, leading eventually to the grassy top of Hollin Ridge, is steep and uneven and in places almost fades out altogether.

We went in procession across the sun-dappled floor of the hollow between the great old trees. Paul was telling Stuart about his previous camping week at Hollin Bank. It had rained every day, he said, and the tents had leaked and the ponies been smothered in mud.

There was not much risk of that this time, I thought. Unless it broke down in thunder we looked set for a week of perfect weather. The holiday week finished with a gymkhana on Friday afternoon when the parents came to fetch them home. And the day after that was Hensingham Show.

At the thought of the show a tingle of excitement ran through me. When the time came I would probably be a bag of nerves, but now the thought of the show in six days' time cast a happy glow over the week. There were a million things that could go wrong – Shasta going lame or developing a cough; drenching rain on the day of the show – but in the green quietness of the woods such things seemed comfortably remote.

Clare, riding at my side on fat little Snowdrop, seemed to read my thoughts for she said shyly, 'I think your horse is lovely. Do you ride her at shows?'

'I'm taking her to one on Saturday.'

'I bet she wins,' Clare said loyally.

'I've entered her in the Foxhunter class. It's nothing to do with fox-hunting,' I explained, seeing a puzzled expression cloud her face. 'It's a class for young horses just coming into show-jumping. You get Foxhunter classes at shows all over the country, then the finals are held each year at the Horse of the Year Show. It's called after a very famous showjumper called Foxhunter.'

Since coming up out of the hollow we had been walking at an easy pace along a wide bridleway, well spaced out, with Measles and Starshine tagging behind. Now I suddenly realized, looking ahead at the horses in front, that Lara and Danny were no longer with us.

'We'd better catch up with the others,' I said to Emma and Clare, trying to sound casual and putting Shasta into a trot. Inside I was churning with anxiety, almost panic, as I realized that for the past few minutes I had scarcely noticed the leaders at all. I had been too busy talking to Clare and thinking of the show.

Leaving the younger ones behind, I cantered on past Paul and Stuart and Lara's friend Annabel, telling myself that round the next bend I was sure to see Lara.

Deep down I knew all the time that I wouldn't. The next stretch of path, sloping gently down the hill, showed only bare earth and dappled leaves.

I reined in as Stuart cantered up behind. 'Did you see where Lara went? Has she gone on in front?'

Stuart shook his head. 'She dropped behind. I thought she was waiting for you.'

'I'll scalp her when we find her,' I said grimly. Wheeling Shasta round, I came back to Paul and Annabel. 'Have you seen Lara?'

'She's in front somewhere,' they said vaguely.

We stood in a little group on the path. To the rest of them Lara's disappearance was nothing more than a pleasant diversion, adding interest to the ride. 'Lara!' I yelled. 'Lara!'

There was no answer. Here the woodland was more open, tall old trees with plenty of space below. It was impossible for Lara to be out of sight so quickly that no one saw her go! The group of younger ones now joined us, faces alert with excitement. 'What's happened?' they asked.

I thought swiftly. If Danny really *had* bolted with Lara they must surely have been seen. There would have been thudding hooves, cries of alarm. And even if she had sneaked off just to hide from us, it seemed impossible – among these well spaced-out trees – that no one had seen her go. I looked suspiciously at the faces of Annabel and Paul, who gazed back at me with unblinking innocence. 'Well, at least Danny can't have bolted,' I said matter-of-factly, knowing they wanted me to think that he had. Tracey and Sandra ambled up to join us. 'We're just waiting for Lara to come back,' I told them.

For a minute or so there was silence. In the wood nothing stirred.

'Has she gone to the loo or something?' asked Tracey.

Annabel sniggered, but tried to hide it.

'Probably shovelling more eye make-up on,' said Sandra. 'Honestly, have you seen that stuff she puts on her hair?'

She caught Tracey's eye as she spoke and the word 'hair' was lost in giggles.

'I think you ought to go and look for them,' said Paul. 'I bet you anything he's bolted! Lara was finding him really hard to hold.'

This was almost certainly a lie. Every time I had seen Lara she had been urging Danny forward.

But nagging doubts still filled my mind. What if Danny *had* bolted? After all I had scarcely noticed them since we left the hollow. I had let my thoughts wander to Hensingham, to Shasta . . . *Oh God*, I thought in guilty panic, *please show me what to do!* I knew full well that I should have been watching all the time. They were my responsibility.

'Lara!' I shouted into the empty-seeming woodland. 'Lara! Come back at once!'

Behind me, Lara's friend was sniggering again. I knew it, though I couldn't see her. I knew they wanted me to go and look for her.

I was tempted to carry on, leaving Lara to join us when she tired of the joke. I thought we might even find her waiting for us, all innocence and feigned impatience, further down the track. I didn't believe for a moment that she was in trouble.

Yet there was always a chance that she *might* be. And I was responsible for her. I was in a dilemma – if I left the rest here on the path I would probably come back to find that most of them had disappeared too. No doubt it was just what they wanted!

'Are you *sure* none of you saw her leave?'

There were instant protestations of innocence. Nobody had seen a thing.

'Somebody ought to look for her,' Paul said again.

I didn't really have much choice. I swallowed my

pride. 'I'm going to have a quick scout round,' I said. 'You lot stay here — dismount if you like — and rest for a few minutes. I'm putting Stuart in charge, and if anybody wanders off or does anything stupid there'll be big trouble! And while I'm gone you can start thinking where that leather-dressing might be,' I added as a parting shot. They stood, apparently subdued, and watched me go. If she had gone downhill to the right we would come upon her eventually anyway, so I struck off left upwards into the trees, keeping alert for any sound. Very few people rode in this part of the wood. Anyone going to the top of the ridge would use the other path, for the ground here very soon became steep with patches of stone and brambles.

Higher up the trees thinned out and I came upon a more open patch where the earth was damp and soft. I scanned the ground, hoping to find hoofprints. *Oh God, please show me where she is*, I prayed desperately. I think I hoped to be led to where Lara was hiding, perhaps behind a tangle of bushes or one of the thick old yew trees that dotted the woodland. Further up there was a disused cottage. Was she hiding there?

'Lara?' I called.

Suddenly my eye was caught by hoofmarks, quite new and distinct. I reined in and slipped down from the saddle. Yes, a pony's prints, though whether they were Danny's I could not tell. Certainly they had been made today, since the rain. I stood up and scanned the wood. 'Lara!' I shouted again. 'Lara, where are you? Are you all right?'

There was no reply. I gazed again at the prints. They were well spaced as if the pony had been walking. He had perhaps been led, for to one side I found part of a footprint. Why on earth should she want to lead him? After a small area where the turf was worn and muddy the hoofprints died out. Was it worth going further up, towards the cottage?

At least Danny hadn't bolted, I thought with relief. Whatever Lara was up to was deliberate, or she wouldn't have been leading Danny away from us.

'Lara!' I shouted angrily into the wood. 'We're going back. You're spoiling the ride for everyone. Come back to the path and follow us down!'

'I'm on the path already!' The answering shout came from down below.

'Lara, is that you?' I stared down the hillside in disbelief.

'She's here! She's here with us on the path!' There was a chorus of shouts, all brief and excited-sounding as if the shouters had difficulty in restraining their hilarity. I turned Shasta back down the hill.

All the kids were mounted and waiting on the path.

'Where on earth have you been?' I demanded of Lara.

'I went on ahead. When I realized how far behind you all were I came back again.'

'She did come back along the path,' Emma confirmed.

I looked suspiciously at Lara. She stared defiantly back, quite unrepentant.

'All right. We won't waste more time looking into it now. You, Lara, will ride in the middle with Karen and Caroline.'

And let's hope some of Danny's energy rubs off on to Measles, I thought crossly, or Mr Bryant will think we've *all* got lost.

I had planned the ride so that we passed by a farmhouse where teas and ice-cream were sold. In summer the farmer's wife puts out little chairs and tables in the apple orchard to one side of the house and hangs a white-painted sign on the gate. The last part of the ride, since leaving the wood, had been along a country road in the full heat of the sun. By the time we reached the farm everyone was tired and thirsty. There were whoops of delight when we came upon the old brick farm, its front garden bright with sunflowers and hollyhocks and nasturtiums.

'We wouldn't be very popular if we took the ponies to the orchard,' I said, 'though they would probably have a real feast on the apples! We'll have to eat our ice-cream and things out here. At least the verge is wide and shady. If we go up to the house a few at a time, the rest of us can hold the ponies.'

Everyone dismounted. I left Shasta with Stuart and took a few of the younger ones through a low iron gate into the garden while the rest flung themselves down on the cool grass or climbed onto the wall. A door stood open at the side of the house and when we knocked the farmer's wife appeared, plump and rosy in a flowered dress. She was a kind, happy-looking person. She led us into a large kitchen where crisps and chocolate biscuits and slabs of fruit cake and scones with cream and big red strawberries were laid out on the table. A fat brown teapot sat by a simmering kettle. There was ice-cream in the freezer, she told us, and canned drinks in the fridge.

We made our selection and paid our money. The farmer's wife brought out a tub of ice-cream, scooping it into cornets for us, then dipping the cornets into chocolate and nuts. The ice-cream was home-made with thick cream from the farm. She also showed us the water trough in the yard, knowing that the ponies might like a drink too.

The afternoon heat was less intense by the time we left. The ponies stepped out eagerly, sensing home. The ET's were more relaxed, less trouble. Even Lara seemed content to ride with the others and join in the general jokey conversation. As for Measles, he became almost lively, plodding along energetically with his ugly spotty nose turned firmly towards home.

As we neared the stables, I wondered how Rob and Susi and Mrs Gale had done at their shows and whether they were back yet. Soon I'd have to start on evening stables – all those buckets to fill! But at least tonight I'd have help from the ET's. That was part of their training.

Back at the yard we found a green lorry parked over at one side.

'Rob's back!' said Lara, suddenly coming to life.

The ET's pressed forward, eager to greet the returning hero. But both van and cab were empty and the door of Coppernob's box stood open, still awaiting his return. Mr Bryant and a man in green overalls appeared round the corner of the indoor school, coming from the pony-field.

'That's not our lorry,' I said to Lara. 'Coppernob's not home.'

I didn't recognize the lorry. Had we perhaps got a new livery?

I sent the ET's round the back to the row of wooden loose-boxes that we use on holiday weeks and led Shasta to her own box. As I unsaddled I heard cheery voices saying goodbye, the cab door slam shut and the noise of the engine as the lorry was turned round in the yard. When it had gone I heard Mr Bryant's footsteps.

He stood in the doorway, sleeves rolled up on his brown strong-looking arms, his face flushed with the sun. 'Had a good ride? No problems?' he asked kindly.

I hesitated, wondering whether to tell him about Lara. 'The others are up at the bungalow,' he said, moving away from the doorway. 'If you've finished with Shasta come and see the new pony.'

I left my stuff in the tack-room on the way and went with him to the pony-field. Mr Bryant always looks supremely healthy and content with life. As we strolled the short distance from the yard, the late afternoon sun lighting up the fields around us, I thought how lovely it must be to live up here with all the horses and do the job you liked best in all the world. Then I remembered the bank letter. Even Mr Bryant's life had its problems.

But of course if we had got another pony at livery that would bring in more money. I mean, everything helps.

He stopped and rested his arms on the top of the gate. After the first excitement of having a newcomer in their midst, the ponies were now grazing peacefully. I picked out the new pony at once, a liver chestnut standing to our right along by the wall. He saw us and trotted up, thrusting a friendly nose into Mr Bryant's hand. On finding Mr Bryant had no titbits to offer, he turned his attention to me, nuzzling my hand and pockets, lifting his top lip and delicately nibbling my sleeve.

'Hey, stop it!' I said, pushing him away. I found a sugar lump in the very bottom of my pocket. He snaffled it up at once. 'Isn't he friendly?' I said. 'What is his name?'

Mr Bryant stroked the pony's ears. Then he dropped his bombshell. 'He's the one we bought last week with Fandango – don't you remember? This is Double Cherry.'

9

The real Double Cherry

DOUBLE CHERRY! My head was in a whirl. 'But what . . .' I said, then I broke off, confused. If this was Double Cherry, what about that pony which came last week and was shut up in the end box? That is what I wanted to slay. Then I remembered the dye. And Mr Bryant's anger when Sherry had gone near the box.

Double Cherry thrust a friendly nose at me, prodding me for more sugar.

'He's lovely,' I said, my mind racing. Double Cherry *was* lovely. And he must have cost a handsome price!

'Seems to be settling in well,' said Mr Bryant with satisfaction as he turned away from the gate. 'Did you enjoy your ride?'

'Oh yes. Yes.' The ride seemed a million miles away. Glancing back as we left, I saw Double Cherry still standing alertly by the gate.

Despite help from the ET's the evening stablework seemed to last for ever. I couldn't wait to get home and share the news with Chris. If I didn't tell somebody soon I'd burst. With so many ponies already, why should Mr Bryant suddenly buy a new one? Such an expensive-looking one. And what had happened to the mysterious pony that had been dyed?

I was lucky. Chris was not only at home but was doing nothing more demanding than standing by the cooker, watching some beefburgers cook. I said, 'Chuck a couple in for me, will you? I'm ravenous!'

'So what's new?' said Chris. 'You eat like a horse all the time. It must be the company you keep.'

'I'll tell you what's new!' I said. And I told him about Double Cherry — the real Double Cherry — and about the pony that had been kept hidden, with a patch of wet dye on its back. 'And where that one is now,' I said, 'I have no idea. It seems to have vanished as mysteriously as it came. There's something weird going on, I'm sure of it.'

Chris moved the beefburgers around the pan with a fork. He said, 'I don't know what you're worrying about. It's nerves, I expect, with the show and everything. There's nothing *mysterious*, just because they moved the first pony when you weren't there. They don't have to get your permission for everything, you know. Perhaps they were just looking after it for a few days for someone else. And how do you *know* Double Cherry was expensive? He could have been a real bargain. Maybe that's why they bought him.'

'You could be right,' I said. 'On the other hand, so could I.'

'I don't see how you can find out either way. Not without seeing the bill of sale or whatever.' Chris slapped his own beefburgers onto a plate. While mine were cooking I cut hunks off a big crusty loaf, buttered them thickly and piled them with black cherry jam. I made a big mug of hot chocolate then put the beefburgers on a dinner plate with a load of coleslaw and three tomatoes, and cut a big wedge of fruit cake.

'Are you trying to fatten yourself up or something?' asked Chris.

'I always eat a lot when I'm worried.'

'Any excuse,' said Chris companionably. 'I think I'll have some of that cake myself.'

While we were eating Dad came in from church. He looked very fit and healthy after his day's gardening. He saw the frying-pan on the cooker and went to the fridge for bacon.

'It's all right, I'll do it,' I said, jumping up from the table and taking over.

Dad sat down at the table, no doubt surprised by my instant offer.

'Nice to see you earning your living for a change,' Chris said pleasantly.

But really it was my guilty conscience, because when Mum was with us we used to go to church almost every Sunday, all of us. Now it was usually just Dad on his own – if anyone at all. I hadn't meant it to be like that. Somehow it had just happened. 'God may be faithful,' I thought ruefully to myself, 'but I'm afraid *I'm* not!' So instead I made Dad's supper, and when I handed it over and he said, 'Good girl' I felt that praise had seldom been less deserved.

Afterwards we sat round the table for ages and I told them about Lara and the ET's, which was quite hilarious when you came to think of it.

But later, in my room, looking through the open window at the quiet fields, I remembered Double Cherry. 'Oh Lord, please help me,' I said. 'Please bless all my family and help us to do what is right. And thank you for my happy day,' I added, realizing that all my prayers these days seemed to be asking for things.

Then I got into bed, luxuriating in the cool covers and the sheer bliss of stretching out flat after a hard day's work. And in less than a minute I was asleep.

Bright sunlight woke me. It seems that however early you get up in summer the world outside is already wide awake and about its business. Monday, six o'clock.

This morning the ET's were visiting some racing stables twenty miles away with Mr Bryant, and in the afternoon they were to have jumping lessons with Rob. I lay in bed and thought about it. A whole blissful day − after mucking out and feeding − to spend as I liked with Shasta! This morning we might go for a hack before the sun got hot − just to enjoy ourselves, with no pupils or anything to bother about. And later, if the field was free, we might go round the jumps. But I must make sure that Shasta didn't work too hard and that she got her rest day. I would ask Mr Bryant about it, I thought. And I remembered that I would need to have her feet checked when the farrier came.

When I arrived at Hollin Bank that morning, I was greeted by the ET's with the news that Rob had won two seconds the previous day. They pointed with pride to the two blue rosettes pinned over Coppernob's door. Rob himself was in the feed-store, measuring scoops of supplement out of a tin. When I went in he looked up and grinned.

'Congrats,' I said.

'Should have been first in one of them, if I hadn't mucked up the last jump. Ah well, you can't win them all!' he said.

'Not even Coppernob?' I asked, unable to resist a smile.

Rob turned the tin upside-down over Coppernob's feed bowl and banged it with his hand to dislodge the last traces of powder. 'I wonder if Dad remembered to get more supplement.'

'That's the magic formula, is it?'

'It's good stuff. You should get some for Shasta.'

He tossed me the empty tin. All our horses, Shasta included, were given supplement twice a week, but this was a new, superior brand bought specially for Coppernob and Fandango. They had it every day. Except for Shasta, all the liveries had their own tins of supplement, paid for by their owners. As I read the glowing recommendations on the tin I felt a pang of envy. I would certainly have got some for Shasta – if I could have afforded it!

I looked up to find that Rob was watching me. It was embarrassing the way he so often seemed to read my thoughts. He said casually, 'Have you ever thought of selling? We would probably buy her back ourselves, so you would still see her each day. You could get something cheaper – there are lots of fairly good horses about – and have a bit of money in your pocket. Then you could buy the new one anything you wanted.'

I was so startled that I dropped the tin. It clattered and rolled about on the floor while I stared at Rob.

'I would never sell Shasta. Never!'

Rob shrugged. 'Please yourself, of course, but I would have thought it was the obvious thing. Shasta would do well with me. Think about it.'

'Not likely!' I picked up the supplement tin and threw it back to him. 'I'll buy Shasta some out of our first winnings.' I was annoyed by what he was suggesting. Why couldn't he leave me alone?

I started to make up the feeds, following the chart on the feed-store wall – so much oats, so much bran and beet, milk pellets for the ponies, extra nuts for Hollyhock. As if I would let Rob have Shasta! But I *would* have liked to get her the supplement. And should she have more feed now that she was working more, I wondered? I was so anxious to have her in top form for the show.

I finished my work in good time, had a drink with the holiday mob, then saddled up and set out for the woods. I had to slip away quickly, otherwise I would have been landed with Sherry. She has a skin as thick as a rhino's and takes it for granted that when there is a camping holiday she can simply come up and join in. But she hadn't known that the group was going out with the Bryants that morning. I knew that as soon as she realized, she would latch herself onto me and tag along until they returned. But if I managed to leave her behind with Mr Betts she would probably get bored and go home. So I drank my lemonade quickly and set off. By the time Sherry came to the yard to look for me I would be out of sight in the woods!

It was blissful weather for riding. I had planned to take the same route as yesterday. But it was a mistake, for though the woods were just as lovely and the shade as inviting, I could scarcely enjoy it at all. Everything I saw brought back the events of the previous day – and especially that moment back at Hollin Bank when Mr Bryant had proudly pointed out Double Cherry.

Then what about the strange pony in the end box? Why had it been dyed? And where was it now?

I puzzled over this as I rode. Before long, the charm went out of the morning. Chris's reassurances now seemed less convincing than ever. true, Mr Bryant *could* have been looking after the pony for someone else. But that didn't explain why the pony had been shut up out of sight. Still less did it explain that suspicious patch of dye.

I went back to the stables by the shorter route, cutting

out the farm where we had bought the ice-cream. As I rode down the track I met Mr Betts coming up towards the bungalow for lunch. He strode up, his cap pulled over his eyes against the sun, and nodded briefly to me as he passed. The stable yard looked bright and deserted, sun dazzling down on the concrete, most of the horses back in the shade of their boxes.

When I had seen to Shasta I wandered with my bag of lunch round the end of the indoor school, where a large leafy tree overhung the path to the pony-field and spires of pink foxgloves grew against the wall. Here I sat down, the pleasant sights and sounds of summer all around me, and unpacked my lunch – tomatoes, cheese sandwiches, two caramel wafers, a bag of crisps and an apple. It was lovely to sit there in the warmth, enjoying having the place to myself. Mr Betts would probably be at the bungalow for hours. Monday was the day our horses rested, so no pupils would be coming. Until evening stables there was nothing much to do.

I drained my can of Coke, which was rather warm, and lay back to relax. Thoughts of the cold drinks machine in the office came into my mind. After a few minutes I sat up, found the right money in my pocket, and went down into the yard. The office door was hardly ever locked. I went in and got myself a drink.

My eyes were drawn to the tall metal cabinet in the corner. If I saw the bill of sale, Chris had said, I would know whether Double Cherry had been an irresistible bargain . . . But I was not going to be caught that way twice! If the only way to solve the mystery was by searching Mr Bryant's confidential papers, then it would have to stay unsolved. No more looking in locked drawers for *me*.

On the other hand, papers left lying openly about on a desk, in an unlocked office . . . Surely there could be no harm in *that*? After all, anyone might see them.

All the same I was taking no chances. I went out into the yard, checked carefully, then came in again and closed the door behind me. I went round to the other side of the desk by the chair and glanced at the scattered papers. All of them seemed innocent. Most of them concerned the camping holiday — letters from parents that had enclosed cheques, instructions from Emma's Mum about her hay fever drops. I slid open the top drawer and there was the key, small and shiny and inviting. I moved it and looked at the papers beneath. Feed bills. The other drawers had things like old ballpoints and pencils, a large brown envelope of rosettes for the gymkhana, bundles of very old papers in elastic bands, a pair of sunglasses and a riding stick which had presumably been left behind at some time by pupils.

If only I had noticed the date on that letter from the bank! It might be *years* old! (And yet if it was years old, why had it been lying about, so new-looking, on the top of the pile?)

I opened the desk drawer again, picked up the key and stood with it in my hand. It would be so easy with no one around . . .

I crossed to the cabinet and fitted the key in the lock. But that was all. I didn't turn it. With determination I thrust the key back on top of the papers and closed the drawer. As I did so I caught a movement at the window.

Total panic hit me. I stood glued to the spot, my heart thudding like a steam engine. It could only be Mr Betts — there was no one else around. I stood trapped, waiting for the door to open. This time there would be no mercy. It was the end for me and Shasta, without a doubt.

When the seconds ticked by and no one came I crossed to the window and looked out at the yard. Only the horses' heads moved, blinking and twitching their ears at their doors. I went out into the yard. It lay hot and still and empty. No one was there at all.

I couldn't believe my luck. Surely if it had been Mr Betts he would have marched straight in and confronted me! Could it have been a bird flitting past, casting a swift shadow? Certainly *something* had moved. But what?

I knew the answer as soon as I got back to my things. Under the shady tree by the foxgloves sat a figure in scruffy jeans. Its lank hair was slicked back behind its ears. It was eating my crisps.

'Hi,' said Sherry conversationally. 'Did you find what you were looking for?'

10

A busy week

'SHERRY!' I exclaimed in astonishment. 'How long have *you* been here?'

'Hours and hours.' Sherry continued to eat the crisps as calmly as if they were her own. 'And dead boring it's been too. I didn't know you were going out for a ride.'

'You could have gone home.'

'That's dead boring as well.' She screwed up the crisp packet and lobbed it over into the pony-field. 'What are we going to do this afternoon?'

'I know what *I'm* going to do. Was it you looking in through the office window just now?'

'Yeh. I was in the tack-room and I saw you come out of the office in a very secretive sort of way, look round, then go in again. So I thought I'd have a squint at what you were up to.'

'I wasn't "up to" anything,' I said, annoyed. How much had Sherry seen? Had she watched me reading the papers on the desk or looking in the drawers? And what if she had only seen the last part, as I replaced the key in the drawer? She would certainly have assumed the worst. 'I was just looking round while I had my drink', I said.

'Of course you were,' she agreed. 'I often do the same myself.'

I looked at her suspiciously to see if she was taking the mickey out of me. With Sherry you can't always tell. She started scrambling to her feet.

'I think I'll get a drink right now,' she said. 'Those crisps have made me thirsty.'

Should I ask her not to tell anyone about what she'd seen? Or would that simply make her suspicious and fix it in her mind? Anyway, why *should* she tell?

'Sherry, if you breathe a word of this I'll slay you.'

'Aw, stop making such a fuss about things. I don't suppose you pinched anything, so who's worrying?'

Who's worrying? Well, I was, for one. I wasn't exactly proud of what I had done and to have been caught in the act by Sherry was especially shaming. And Sherry was so indiscreet. She could let it slip without a second thought.

'Sherry,' I said when she came back, 'I meant what I said. I haven't taken anything, or done anything like that, but if you tell what you've seen I'll never speak to you again.'

'Oh, forget it,' said Sherry. 'Everybody noses about in the office. I once found a real soppy Valentine from Rob to someone called Honeylips. I suppose in the end he hadn't the nerve to send it.'

I wasn't sure that I could forget it myself. But at least, with a bit of luck, Sherry would. She had a dreadful memory even for things she *ought* to remember, I reminded myself comfortingly.

It was a busy mixed-up sort of week, with the

ET's and everything. I had hoped that Shasta wouldn't have too much work, especially as I was riding her more than usual myself. But on two evenings that week she was out on hacks with adult riders, and on Tuesday afternoon I arrived to find her being galloped round the indoor school by the most clueless ham-fisted idiotic girl you could imagine, who seemed to think she was some sort of circus act or rodeo rider. When I stopped her she said she was waiting to have a jumping lesson.

Meanwhile Rob was having problems with Fandango, who had developed a cough. Sue Kettlewell came up to the stables to see the invalid and watch Rob put Coppernob through his paces. Coppernob was certainly in fine form. It was unnerving to think that on Saturday Shasta and I would be competing against them at Hensingham.

By Wednesday I was a bag of nerves. Rob and Sue had built a course based on last year's Foxhunter course. After they had gone I took Shasta round and knocked nearly half of it down.

'That was terrible,' I said to Wendy, who had come to watch. 'Rob says I ought to push her on more, use my stick. Perhaps he's right.'

'I don't know about using your stick, but you certainly need a more positive approach. If you calmed down it would help,' she said.

'I can't. I've got too much on my mind,' I wailed.

'Are you taking anyone with you? Chris? Your father? You ought to have someone to give you a hand. Or what about Sherry? It would help you relax too. It's a pity Rob won't have room in the lorry this time. I believe they need the third space for Bay Robin.' Bay Robin was Mrs Bryant's show hunter.

'I don't mind hacking there. I'm going to start early. The Foxhunter is at half past ten.'

It was seven miles to Hensingham. Chris or Dad –

I hadn't asked them yet – would go by car and meet me there. Then they could watch me making a fool of myself knocking down all the fences, I thought glumly, as Wendy and I went round replacing all the poles.

That muddled, busy week went all too quickly. On Thursday evening, their last at Hollin Bank, the ET's were to have a barbecue. From the purely social point of view the barbecue was the high spot of the holiday. The equestrian high spot came the following afternoon, in what was referred to on their programme as a Grand Gymkhana. For the barbecue Mr Bryant had bought coloured lights to string between the trees. There would be music, and Wendy and her husband were coming to help with the cooking. The last night in camp was always a great time for apple-pie beds and frogs in sleeping-bags. Thank goodness I would be out of the way when they started that sort of thing!

Everybody was in the mood for a party that day – except me. Work was the last thing in their minds. After breakfast I was supposed to show them how to plait and get a pony ready for a show. Even John and James were late down to the yard because they wanted to watch the barbecue being set up. The plaiting and grooming were got through with a great deal of fooling about. I was glad when it was time to finish.

'Well, I hope you'll all remember what you've learned,' I said, as we helped ourselves from the box of fizzy drinks that had been left outside the office. 'It's going to be judged by Wendy and she's quite strict. There's also a prize for the best kept loose-box. She's been checking on that all week.'

I sat down on the bench outside the office. Emma and Clare, drinks in hand, immediately sat down next to me. 'There's a prize for the person who's made most progress, too,' Clare said earnestly. 'It's a special rosette, I've seen it. Oh, I do hope I win it!'

I would have liked her to win it, too. She was very

sweet, and so hard-working. She had slaved over Snowdrop all week. The trouble was that she *had* done it all week, so that her efforts could hardly be described as 'progress'. Sadly for Clare, the prize was most likely to go to one of the beginners.

'At my last camp here I got four rosettes,' said Paul, making sure that everyone heard.

'Bet they weren't red or blue,' said Lara

'Well, I bet I get more than you tomorrow,' Paul retorted.

'Gymkhanas are for kids,' she said, pushing back her hair and giving him a petulant stare, 'so you probably will.'

'Lara would rather have a kiss from you-know-who,' Tracey murmured to Sandra, and the two of them collapsed into giggles.

'Well, I may be unobservant, but I *don't* know who,' I said.

Stuart, with an air of unconcern, began to sing 'Robbie is my darling, my darling, my darling . . .'

'Shut up!' Lara said fiercely.

Come on,' I said, 'if you've finished we ought to be getting back to work. Put your empty tins in the bin. I'm going to get Shasta and show you how to wash a horse. We'll need the shampoo from the tack-room.'

'Did you ever find that leather-dressing?' Tracey asked innocently. Then she caught Sandra's eye and they exploded into giggles, which they tried to hide by racing off towards the tack-room.

'What a couple of wallies,' said Lara's friend Annabel, watching them go. 'They'll never be proper riders if they try until they're a hundred. They ought to stick to Space Hoppas or Kiddicars.'

Sandra and Tracey came back with the shampoo. I hosed Shasta down and they all watched as I set to work. I suppose it wasn't a particularly fascinating spectacle, but Mr Bryant had put it down on their programme so we had to make the best of it. I explained what I was doing, trying to make it as interesting as possible, while Lara and Annabel watched everything I did with an air of critical expertise and the rest just stood about in assorted attitudes of boredom. If I had been a bit more quick-witted I would have asked Lara and Annabel to do the washing while *I* stood by and criticized. 'Seven out of ten,' said Lara to Annabel when I had finished. I could have sloshed them.

'Now Wendy's going to give you a talk on saddlery, the proper fitting of saddles and things like that,' I said, wondering why all the boring-sounding things had been left to this morning.

'Not us,' said Lara at once. 'We've arranged to have a private jumping lesson until lunch-time.'

'But we're *all* going to do jumping this afternoon,' I protested.

'So what? This is just for us, in the indoor school.'

They were welcome to the indoor school as far as I was concerned. It was like an oven in the middle of the day, even though the doors were permanently open. The rest of us went to the tack-room where Wendy was sitting, perched on the edge of the table, waiting for us. She had brought a half-made saddle to show them, with the tree and all the framework exposed. She showed us how the stitching was done, first marking the rows of holes with a sort of sharp-toothed comb, so that they were evenly spaced, then pushing the holes right through one by one with a bradawl. It was done with two needles at a time, crossing each other from front to back. Then she showed us different types of nosebands and bits and why well-fitting tack was important.

It was interesting, but by lunch-time everyone had had enough of stablework and was longing to get on with some riding.

When we arrived back at the bungalow for lunch, we found Lara and Rob already there. The day was hot.

Lara, smart and neat in boots, jodhs and open-necked shirt, sat coolly in the shade while Rob poured her a drink. The rest of us — an inferior rabble in tee-shirts, jeans and trainers — piled round the tables and grabbed for the lunch-boxes and cups. We had scarcely started eating when Sherry appeared. She edged herself on the end of one of the benches, put a bag of sandwiches on the table and reached for a cup. One of the lunch-boxes still remained unopened.

'Who hasn't got their lunch?' I asked.

'I'll have it!' volunteered Paul at once.

'It can't be spare. There must be someone missing.' I glanced round the table, at Rob and Lara sitting beneath the tree. 'Where's Annabel?' I called to Lara.

Lara, pausing between mouthfuls, looked unconcerned. 'She went into the house. She wanted help to get her boots off.' Lara turned her attention back to Rob and her Cornish pasty.

It was another five minutes before Annabel came to claim her lunch. She still wore the boots. 'Mrs Bryant says they'll probably come off more easily when I've cooled down,' she said as she went across to join Rob and Lara. 'Anyway it's probably not worth it. We'll be riding again in half an hour.' She sat down on the grass and tugged the lid off her lunch-box.

'I'd laugh if those two won no gymkhana prizes at all,' said Stuart.

'They're bound to. They've been practising every minute and they've got the best ponies,' said someone.

'And the biggest heads,' said Paul.

When he said 'Biggest heads' Sandra and Tracey, who were drinking, exchanged glances and spluttered into their lemonade.

After we had finished eating and everything was cleared up, the ET's trooped off with Mr Bryant. I was relieved to see that Sherry was tagging along too. She had no pony to ride and would no doubt make herself useful by putting up jumps and so on. But at least she wouldn't be trailing around after me.

As this thought crossed my mind, so did the fear I had been keeping at bay ever since I had asked for a friend. 'Oh, God, please don't let it be Sherry!' I muttered fervently as I went back to the yard to get Shasta. 'Okay, perhaps she isn't so bad, and perhaps she needs a friend too. But please don't let it be *me*!'

Anyway, now that I was so busy at the stables the longing for a friend had become less urgent. In fact, as I left the ET's squealing and chasing about the yard and set out across the fields, I reflected that solitude had a lot going for it.

Shasta had had a busy week so I decided not to take her far. For a time we galloped and cantered, enjoying our freedom, drinking in the warmth and quietness of the countryside. Woods and harvest fields lay all about, and below in the valley the combine harvesters moved about the fields like toys.

Then back to Hollin Bank for a final go at the jumps with Wendy.

The ET's didn't help with evening stables that day. They were too busy at their camp behind the bungalow, getting ready for the barbecue. But Wendy stayed behind and helped. Her husband Richard was coming up later.

'I hope everything goes off all right,' I said, collecting my bike when we had finished.

'You're not going home, are you?'

'I certainly am. I'm dead beat. Besides Chris has hired a video I want to see.'

'Oh, what a pity! See you tomorrow then. Oh I say,' she called after me, 'would you mind calling at the bungalow and telling Mrs Bryant I put the burgers in the freezer? She wasn't there when I came past.'

The Bryants' back garden had a carnival air. Music

92

was playing, and Mr Bryant – looking quite out of character in a red and blue striped apron – was lighting the barbecue. 'Is Mrs Bryant in the house?' I asked.

He nodded curtly but didn't speak. Not very friendly really. I put it down to the fact that he was busy.

The holidaymakers were darting around from tent to tent in various stages of undress, or parading in and out of the back door with towels and dripping hair. John Digsby-whatsit was zooming about the grass on a bike. Stuart was tuning his guitar. Lara and Annabel had somehow fixed a mirror onto the outside of a tent and were arranging one another's hair with the aid of setting mousse. The tables had been moved to one side and Rob was putting out forks and paper plates. He was wearing an expensive new shirt, bought with money borrowed from his mother. Annabel, I noticed, still wore her riding boots.

'Wendy said the burgers are in the freezer,' I said, finding Mrs Bryant in the kitchen. She was tipping tins of fruit into a huge bowl to make fruit salad.

'Yes, thanks. I found them. Will you be a love and put this in the fridge while I get Emma's medicine?'

In the end it was half past seven by the time I reached home. On the way there I met Sherry – face freshly scrubbed, hair sleeked back, wearing a blouse that had once been mine – bent double over the handlebars as she forced Chris's bike slowly up the hill to Hollin Bank.

'Why don't you go home to change and come back again?' Mrs Bryant had said when I left. 'It seems a pity to miss all the fun.'

But by the time I had pushed my bike up the brick path to our door I had had enough. I showered, put on my pyjamas and sat down in front of the telly with Chris and a pile of toast.

I knew I would hear all about the barbecue tomorrow – every gruesome detail.

11

The gymkhana – and after

THE NEXT MORNING was once more bright and sunny. The fields beyond my window had the familiar dewy look of early morning, the air was fresh and cool.

Tomorrow, I thought, Shasta and I will be passing here on our way to Hensingham. The thought sent a shiver of excitement through me.

As I dressed I pictured the big show-field. Today they would be putting up the great marquees, marking out the show-rings, fencing off rows and rows of pens for sheep and pigs and cattle and goats. Lorries would arrive stacked with trestle tables, benches for spectators, crates of food and drink for the refreshment tents. And all over the county and beyond farming people and horsy people would be getting started on their day's work, planning ahead as I was for the show.

It was going to be a busy day at Hollin Bank. Because the Bryants and Wendy and I would all be away at the show, tomorrow's pupils had been switched to today or Monday. Then there was the Grand Gymkhana and the departure of the ET's. Their parents were coming to watch the gymkhana and take them home. Mrs Bryant would take a table down to the field and serve refreshments, while Mr Bryant, Rob and Wendy did the judging and organizing. Mr Betts always set up the courses and I was the general dogsbody. It would be a busy day all right. But at least I wouldn't have time to be nervous.

As I pedalled gaily along in the sunshine I never dreamed how differently the day would end.

When I left the road and jolted past the gate of the bungalow the curtains were still closed and the camp behind was quiet. But Rob and his father were already down at the yard. Rob was filling water buckets and Mr Bryant was in the feed-store mixing feeds.

I got Shasta's bucket and he said, 'You'd better open another sack of oats. There's not much left in that one.'

Since I had mentioned Shasta's diet to Rob, she had been fed mostly oats with a bit of beet for flavour.

'I ought to pay you extra,' I had said, 'now she's being fed more oats.'

'But you are doing more work,' he had said without hesitation, rejecting my offer.

The Bryants were always so kind to me. They took as much interest in Shasta as if she was their own. I felt as though I could never repay them for it.

'How did the barbecue go?' I asked, meeting Rob in the yard.

Rob said cheerfully, 'Very well, though there was a bit of a commotion in the night. Dad had to go out in the early hours to put up a tent again. You'd be getting your beauty sleep by then.'

'I needed it, I can tell you! I was just about all in. I'm hoping to be here about five tomorrow, by the way. I want to leave at seven.'

'Yes, it's going to be an early start all round. Mum's hunter class is at half past eight. Mrs Gale is going to an Event and wants Caprice got ready for six-thirty. I'm sorry we can't take Shasta in the lorry.'

'That's all right. How's Fandango this morning, by the way?' As soon as I had said it I wished that I hadn't. Supposing he thought that I hoped Fandango couldn't go, so there would be room for Shasta?

Luckily Rob didn't seem to notice. He said, 'She's fine. Cough's gone completely. It was Dad who realized what the trouble was — some of those kids had been giving her dry hay. Dry hay!' He cast his eyes heavenwards in a gesture of despair.

'You'll be sorry to see them go, though,' I said, thinking of Lara.

When I joined the campers for their eight o'clock breakfast, I thought at first they were quieter because they were tired. Then I realized there was a certain amount of bad feeling about and that Lara was eating on her own. 'Where's Annabel?' I asked her, trying to be friendly.

Lara looked up briefly from her scrambled egg. 'Get lost,' she said.

'Annabel isn't very well,' explained Emma in her piping little voice.

'Sick with love,' said Harriet.

'She wasn't at the barbecue either,' James told me. 'At least, only the first half-hour.'

'We all know what's the matter with *her*,' Paul said. 'She's scared, that's what.'

'I don't see why she should be scared,' I said, helping myself to scrambled egg from the dish in the middle of the table.

'Scared she won't win any prizes this afternoon, so she's pretending to be ill.'

'Oh, don't be so stupid!' Lara slammed her knife and fork down onto the table with a great clatter. She got up from the table and marched towards the bungalow. 'She needs time, that's all,' she called over her shoulder. 'She'll be up by this afternoon for the gymkhana and you lot can expect the thrashing of your lives!'

'What's all *that* about?' I asked when she had gone.

A dozen eager voices began to explain. It seemed that in the early hours of the morning Stuart and Paul, still full of high spirits, had crept out in the darkness and pulled out the tent pegs holding Lara's and Annabel's tent, so that the whole thing had collapsed on top of them. The two girls had gone angrily to demand help from Mr Bryant. Smothered laughter from the boys' tent had given them away. Paul and Stuart were given a thorough telling-off by Mr Bryant and made to put up the tent again. Annabel and Lara, however, were out for revenge. When the campers had woken that morning, they found Stuart's guitar daubed all over with nail varnish and floating in the water trough.

'But that's awful!' I said, appalled. 'It's probably ruined for good! What did they say when you found it?'

'Annabel wasn't there, but Lara said Stuart deserved it. She said this was meant to be a serious riding holiday and people who only came to fool around made her sick.'

'Then Stuart said that if she and Annabel were serious riders, he was Father Christmas,' said Shonna. 'Anyway it ended up with Lara challenging the rest of us put together to get as many rosettes in the gymkhana as her and Annabel.'

'Only Annabel is hiding in the bungalow,' said Paul. 'They're chickening out, that's what. Pretending to be ill.'

Lara didn't join us when we went down to the yard. Presumably she was comforting the suffering Annabel. I was glad she didn't come. Without her the others became more cheerful and the morning's work was done enthusiastically. They all wanted to do well and show their parents how much progress they had made. The incident of the guitar was forgotten for a while.

Break-time came and Lara and Annabel still had not joined us.

'I don't think it's fair that they should miss all the work,' complained Sandra as we helped ourselves to drinks.

'They'll be here before long. They have to get their ponies ready.'

'Do you think they *will* get more prizes than we do?' asked Clare.

'I suppose it's possible. If you're only counting firsts, seconds and thirds.'

'Well, I hope there are lots of classes for under elevens,' said Sandra, 'and then they've had it.'

'I'm not going ot worry about them,' said Debbie. 'They can have the Black Death for all I care.'

'Oh, come on,' said John. 'It's probably only a headache or toothache.'

As the morning wore on Annabel's mystery illness intrigued me more and more. I left the ET's to their grooming and went up the lane to the bungalow.

As I approached, Rob pulled up in his car. He jumped out and slammed the door.

'Just been to Tychwell for more ice-cream,' he said. 'Have they done it yet?'

'Done it?' Done what? I wondered. Pulled her tooth out? Lanced her boil? Pumped out her stomach?

From the high frosted window of the bathroom came a sharp wail.

'Evidently not,' he said.

We went round to the back door and through the kitchen into the hall. The bathroom door was open. Inside the most extraordinary sight met my eyes.

In the bath sat Annabel, fully clothed. She was presumably sitting in cold water for she was shivering, and screaming at Lara to stop and fetch a doctor. By the taps stood Lara. Her face red with exertion, she tugged with all her strength at Annabel's booted foot while Annabel clung to the side of the bath for support, thrashing and rolling like a stranded porpoise.

The struggle must have been going on for some time. The mirror, walls, tiles and everything in sight were running with water. The thick pink towels lay trampled on the floor.

'Get out!' screamed Lara when she saw me.

Near the front door Mrs Bryant was putting down

the telephone. Her free hand held a large pair of scissors. She went to the bathroom with an air of purpose.

'I managed to get your parents at last. They were just leaving to come here,' she said to Annabel. 'They told me to go ahead.'

Then snip-snip went the scissors, slowly and painfully pushing their way down the length of Annabel's smart new boot. Lara saw me watching and slammed the door.

I don't know how the news got round but by lunchtime it was the chief topic of conversation.

'She's had them on since yesterday morning!'

'She couldn't get them off so she just left them.'

'You should just see her legs. They're swollen up big as balloons!'

'They've gone all black and purple.'

'That's probably dye from off the boots,' said James practically.

No one seemed particularly sorry for Annabel. 'Serves her right for messing up Stuart's guitar,' was the general opinion.

Mr Bryant, who had no sympathy for Annabel at all, told us the full story. Mrs Bryant and Lara had struggled to remove the boots the previous evening but after being called to the phone for some time and then hearing nothing further, Mrs Bryant assumed that the boots had been got off by someone else. Annabel had left the barbecue early, hoping rest would make her feet less painful but this morning, while everyone still slept, she had hobbled in agony to the bungalow to ask Mrs Bryant's help. Mrs Bryant had tried to reduce the swelling by making Annabel sit with her booted feet in cold water for an hour and had squirted washing-up liquid down the tops. But the wet boots had gripped her legs more tightly than ever and Annabel had wept with pain and frustration.

'She couldn't get them off yesterday lunch-time,' I

said, remembering. 'Her feet must have been starting to swell then!'

'She should have told us, we would have helped,' said Debbie.

'She didn't want us to know how stupid she is,' said Paul. None of us had any sympathy for Annabel.

As we finished lunch we saw Rob, Lara and Annabel come out of the bungalow and set off down the lane. Both girls wore trainers. Annabel seemed no worse for her experience, unlike her boots.

'They must be going to get their horses ready,' said Sandra. 'It's not fair if they're having Rob to help them.'

'They must have had some lunch with the Bryants,' Stuart said. Their two lunch-boxes were still unopened.

Because of all the fuss with Annabel and the preparation of refreshments for the afternoon, our own lunches had been somewhat scanty.

Mrs Bryant came out to help clear up. One of our tables had to go down to the field.

'How's Annabel?' I asked.

'Oh, fine now, the silly girl. I'm lending her some boots of mine for the gymkhana.'

'Trust *her* to fall on her feet,' said Paul.

The ET's now began to change and get ready. Ties were unearthed from the bottoms of rucksacks. There was a shoe-cleaning box by the back door and a great cleaning of boots began. Clare burst into tears because someone had smeared toothpaste on her shirt.

'Come into the kitchen and I'll rub it off.'

While we were at the sink Annabel and Lara came back. They passed through the kitchen carrying towels and sponge-bags and didn't speak to us. They went into the bathroom and locked the door.

'There, the wet patch will soon dry out,' I said to Clare. 'I hope you do well in the gymkhana and win a rosette to take home.'

She smiled at me and ran out to join the crowd round the polishing-box.

Now the parents were starting to arrive. Unfamiliar cars jolted down the lane on their way to the yard.

'It can't be *that* time!' cried Tracey in horror.

'Don't panic. We don't start for over half an hour. Lara and Annabel are still washing their hair.'

Sandra and Tracey, both trying at once to look in the mirror fixed up by Lara, stopped jostling one another and turned to look at me.

'What's that you said?' asked Tracey.

'They're washing their hair.'

'Oh, glory!' They clung to one another, helpless with laughter. Tears streamed down their faces.

'Can we all share the joke?'

Sandra and Tracey waved their arms uselessly. They couldn't speak.

James Digsby-whatsit said suddenly 'There's our car!' He and John ran to the fence and waved vigorously to a huge blue car that was turning into the lane. It slowed down and a lady in the passenger seat waved to them. The boys ran to get their hats, then followed the car down the lane.

When everyone was ready – except Annabel and Lara, who were presumably still doing wonderful things to their hair – we went down the lane to saddle up. The yard seemed full of parked cars.

In the large paddock the parents sat on picnic chairs. Wendy stood, notebook in hand, to judge the best turned-out pony. Sherry was counting potatoes into buckets. Mr Betts, tall and gaunt in his tilted cap, strode around directing everyone.

Mr Bryant came into the yard. 'Right, kids,' he said, rubbing his hands. This is your big moment. All correctly mounted?' He cast a practised eye over them. 'Get into line then and you can file in.'

'But Lara and Annabel aren't here,' I said.

Mr Bryant glanced at his watch. 'We'll give them a couple of minutes.'

It was almost ten minutes before they appeared. Their faces were like thunder. They went to fetch Danny and Sailor and joined us with a very bad grace.

'Hurry up, we're waiting,' said Mr Bryant. 'I'd have thought you two had caused enough trouble for one day.'

'It's not *us* causing trouble,' snapped Lara.

'They were only washing their hair,' said Tracey. But she was careful not to look at Sandra.

'I wonder what happened to that leather-dressing?' murmured Sandra innocently.

The gymkhana went like a dream. The sun shone, the ponies behaved beautifully, the ET's – miraculously transformed into angels – trotted proudly about the field with rosettes pinned to their sleeves, the parents clapped and admired their children and ate ice-cream. It was one of the best gymkhanas we had ever had.

It was nearly perfect – except for Annabel and Lara's performances. Their frantic efforts to rid their hair of the disgustingly oily leather-dressing (substituted for the shampoo in Lara's bottle by Sandra and Tracey) had not improved their tempers a bit. Neither had Mr Bryant's displeasure over the boots. Their irritation conveyed itself to their ponies. Danny, who could be a real pig when he chose, bucked and pranced and wouldn't do a thing Lara asked him. Sailor barged about knocking into other ponies and kicking up his heels. The two girls got murmurs of sympathy from the spectators but they didn't get many rosettes.

The progress prize was won jointly by John and James. Clare, small and earnest, watched sadly as the beautiful gold and silver rosettes were put into their hands. Her attention was so firmly fixed on them that she didn't hear her own name being called. Wendy had to repeat it: 'Award for the best turned-out pony and rider, Clare Crockford.' Then Clare marched forward with a huge smile on her freckled face and all the other ET's clapped her like mad.

By half past four the gymkhana was over. Parents and children straggled back up the lane to the tents to gather up their belongings. Rob started collecting up the chairs. A traffic jam formed in the lane.

I hate the end of a camp. It is sad to see everybody leave, even if they have been a pain. And I couldn't even go and say goodbye up at the camp, as Wendy did, because it was time for evening stables.

I started to collect the water buckets. Soon Sherry joined me. 'Mr Bryant said he'll be down in ten minutes,' she told me. 'I've come to give you a hand.'

The horses round the yard, excited by the comings and goings, were looking over their doors, ears alert. 'What's all this?' they seemed to say. 'What's going on?' Some banged on their doors, demanding food. Sherry and I staggered from tap to box with heavy buckets. I had no idea that Mr Betts was there as well.

He appeared at the office door and glanced about the yard. 'Where's everyone got to?' he demanded of Sherry.

'Mr Bryant will be down in ten minutes.'

'Good. Let's hope he's got the key.'

'What key?'

It was Sherry who asked the question. Struck dumb with horror I stood rooted to the spot at the other side of the yard.

'The key to the filing cabinet. I know it was here at the week-end.'

I wanted to cry out, to dash across the yard. It was like a bad dream. There was nothing I could do.

'Perhaps Kate put it back in the wrong drawer,' Sherry said helpfully. 'She was using it on Monday.'

12

Prisoners

I HAVE NEVER IN MY WHOLE LIFE seen anyone so furious. Dismissing Sherry, he summoned me into the office and shut the door.

'So, you've been at it again!'

I stood trembling by the drinks machine. Mr Betts' face was dark and angry.

'I didn't look in the filing cabinet. Truly I didn't!'

'Of course you did. She saw you.'

'I just took the key out of the drawer and put it back again.'

'Look here, you. I'm fed up of you snooping about the place! And what have our affairs to do with you anyway, I'd like to know? Now get out of this place. For good. My sister and her husband have done a lot for you over the last two years. What a way to repay them!'

'But I didn't *do* anything. I *didn't*! I was going to, but I changed my mind.'

'Get out of here!'

Angrily he stepped past me to open the door. My eyes blurred with tears. In just a few seconds I would be out in the yard – all my happy times at Hollin Bank finished and done with!

I pulled myself together. 'Wait! I'll tell you all about it,' I said desperately, feeling I had nothing more to lose.

'Come on, then. It had better be good.'

I told him about the stolen Roxy, about the way it tied up with Rainbow. It sounded stupid when I said it out loud. I told him about the pony with the patch of dye, about how I had wanted to reassure myself by looking for a receipt or something. (And what business was it of mine, after all? Oh, what an idiot I'd been!) How I'd accidentally seen the letter from the bank, though not the date on it . . . It sounded completely pathetic, as if I had been reading some trashy magazine. I half expected to hear his scornful, barking laugh.

But Mr Betts was not laughing. His face was dark as thunder. I thought he was going to strike me. 'You vermin!' he hissed. And his eyes blazed with rage.

And then – sickeningly – I knew. I knew beyond any doubt. He was angry because it was true. It was all true. He was raging at me, saying horrible things, but I scarcely heard because the bottom was dropping out of my world. Mr Bryant was a thief. And what about Mrs Bryant? . . . Mr Betts? . . . Rob?

Blindly I turned to the door. Mr Betts grabbed me by the shoulder. 'Don't you dare say a word of this to *anyone*!' he said harshly.

Out of my misery a small flame of defiance flared. 'I'm going to tell the police,' I said with determination.

Mr Betts swung me round. His face came suddenly into focus, staring straight into mine. 'All right,' he said menacingly. 'All right, you do just that. And at the same time ask them something else. Ask where your precious Shasta came from!'

Somehow I was on my bike pedalling blindly up the lane, stones and dry earth rolling backwards beneath my front wheel. Big sobs choked me. My head thudded with a single overwhelming thought. Shasta. Shasta was stolen. She wasn't really mine. Shasta wasn't mine.

Everything I had dreamed of, taken for granted, was in ruins. *Shasta wasn't mine*. As I bumped up the lane I heard a voice call, 'Your back wheel's fallen off!' One of the ET's still around. I kept my head down, hoping they wouldn't see my ravaged face. Then I turned the corner and was out onto the road. Tarmac. Hedges. The golden beauty of a summer evening.

Shasta wasn't mine. Now I knew, it seemed to me I had guessed it all along – ever since Mr Bryant had sold her to me without even knowing her qualities as a jumper. Somehow I had always known there was something wrong. But I had ignored those suspicions, thinking only of the future.

If only – if only I had never read that letter!

I cycled numbly onwards over the quiet sunlit roads. As I cycled, my mind gradually cleared. Jumbled thoughts began to put themselves in order.

Tomorrow's show. How could I ride Shasta, who wasn't mine? But who was going to know she wasn't mine, unless I told them? Perhaps I could tell the police tomorrow evening, after the show? Then I could ride her first. Perhaps, really and truly, I needn't tell at all. I had no facts to support me so what good could it do?

In fact, the police would most likely not even believe me. If I didn't tell I could still stay on at Hollin Bank. Still have Shasta. So what was I worrying about? I thought.

Except for the nagging voice of conscience.

I whizzed round a corner and nearly went slap into a car. The driver's startled face shot by close to my elbow. A split second sooner and I'd have been riding on the bonnet!

I slowed down. Suddenly I felt quite weak and tearful. It was no good. I would have to tell. However much I tried to persuade myself that nothing could be done, I knew with a feeling of dull certainty that it wasn't true. Most likely proof *could* be found. It was my duty to go to the police. Even if it meant losing Shasta.

I gulped. Tears flowed down my face. 'Oh, God, please show me what to do!' I had said. Well, now I knew, and it made me sick with misery.

To reach the police station at Tychwell I would have to pass our house so it seemed sensible to go in and tidy myself up a bit first. I wheeled my bike up the path and, before going in, dried my face and combed my hair in case Dad or Chris were around.

The living-room was empty but Chris was in the kitchen. I tiptoed past and crept up the stairs.

'That you, kiddo?'

'Yes. Down in a minute.'

I felt better when I had washed my face. I wasn't looking forward to this visit to the police station. My only thought now was to get it over with.

'There's tea in the pot,' Chris said when I came downstairs.

'I was just going out.'

Chris was already pouring me a cup. He nodded towards the magazine that lay by it on the kitchen table. 'I collected your mag.'

I wasn't interested in magazines. I considered telling Chris what had happened but decided it would take too long. I was beginning to get quite trembly and wanted to get the whole thing over with. Afterwards, I would come home, fling myself on my bed and let the tears flood out.

'Do you remember that letter?' Chris said.

'Letter?'

'About the stolen pony.'

My heart missed a beat.

Chris pointed to the magazine with his fork. 'There's a letter about it. That pony you told me about. It's been found.'

I could have wept with relief. There it was on the 'Letters' page – Sarah Richardson from Gwent, thanking readers for all the messages and help she had

107

received, and saying that Roxy was now found and safely back in his field! Dazed, happy and bewildered, I could scarcely take it in.

Because it wasn't only wonderful news for Sarah Richardson. It was also wonderful news for me. This whole business had started because of Roxy and Rainbow – the identical markings, the coincidence of dates. Take away the Roxy-Rainbow tie-up and what was left? A letter from a bank saying that at some date Mr Bryant had been having financial problems; a pony that had a patch of dye (And where was that pony now? Gone without proof or trace!); Rob buying a new horse that *I* thought they couldn't afford; an assertion about Shasta made in anger, in order to hurt me: that was all. It was hardly convincing proof. Now that Rainbow was definitely not Roxy the whole case collapsed.

'Oh, Chris!' I cried. 'That's fantastic! I can't tell you why, but it *is*.' I jumped up and hugged him.

Chris was taken by surprise. He nearly choked. 'Have you gone bananas or something? Or are you excited because of the show?'

Hensingham Show! It had gone completely from my mind. There was no reason now for me not to ride Shasta there. Mr Betts, I was sure, had spoken out of spite. Come to that, I would have been angry myself to find someone snooping in my things.

I blushed with shame. If Mr Betts had told, what must they all think of me up there?

'I meant to clean my tack tonight, ready for the show. There'll be enough to do in the morning with Shasta!'

'Oh yes?' Chris put a slice of ham on his bread and folded it in half.

'Well, I was wondering if you would come with me.'

'What on earth for?' Chris looked up in astonishment. For about the eighth time that day I was close to tears.

Chris seemed to understand at once. 'OK. We'll have to cycle, though. Doris's battery is on charge. We'll go as soon as I've finished and if you tell me what to do I'll give you a hand. Here, have some ham and pickle while you wait.'

I found I was really hungry, and supplemented the ham and pickle sandwiches with chocolate biscuits, sponge cake, three jam tarts and a scotch egg. Chris added more tea and water to the pot. It was almost eight by the time we had finished. After eating all that, I didn't much fancy cycling.

'If Dad was here he could have put our bikes in the van and taken us up,' said Chris, obviously feeling much as I did. 'He was here when I came home but he had his tea and went out again. He'll probably be late. He wants to get this job finished off so that he can go to the show tomorrow.' Chris collected his bike from where Sherry had left it by the fence. 'Oh well, I suppose we can take it easy.'

When I thought about it, I was glad that we wouldn't be at Hollin Bank until late. The day's work would be over, the yard empty. I wouldn't have to face the Bryants until tomorrow, when all thoughts would be centred on the show. And perhaps, I thought hopefully, they'll put my odd behaviour down to nerves.

Our tyres whirred softly over the warm tarmac. One side of the road had a broad ribbon of hedge-shadow while the rest lay in yellow sunlight. As the road swung round and began to climb through trees I told Chris about Annabel's boots and how they had washed their hair with greasy leather-dressing. When the road became too steep to cycle we walked in single file.

The hurtling lorry took us by surprise. Down the hill it came, almost filling the narrow road. I shrank back against the hedge. The horse-box shot past us down the hill.

'That's the Hollin Bank lorry!' I said, watching it disappear round the bend. 'But where . . . ?'

'Somebody's in a hurry,' said Chris. 'What a way to drive! Was that Rob?'

'I don't know. I didn't see.'

'Pity the poor horses,' said Chris.

'They wouldn't be taking horses at that speed. Or at this time of day.' I broke off. Why use the lorry if they *weren't* taking horses? Why not the Landrover, or Rob's car? Why such a rush?

'Oh no!' I said. Fear swept through me like a cold tide. 'Chris, there may be something wrong. Dreadfully wrong. We'd better hurry!'

They were moving out the stolen ponies. Mr Betts didn't know I had changed my mind about the police. They were moving ponies out, just in case. And horses too, no doubt. Perhaps Shasta . . .

Oh God, please let Shasta still be there!

In a few words I told Chris what had happened. I had no idea what we would do when we arrived. All I knew was that we must get to Hollin Bank as quickly as possible. There was no one in sight at the bungalow or in the lane. They must all be down at the yard. What would they say to me? What could I say to them?

'I think we should get the police,' Chris said, suddenly braking in the lane.

'But Shasta? What if they're taking Shasta?'

'They wouldn't do that even if she *was* stolen. It would be like admitting guilt.'

'Oh Chris, you must hurry! You don't know what Mr Betts is like. They'll never forgive me for this. They'd take her away even if she *wasn't* stolen. It's their only way of hitting back! If she's still there I'm going to take her away myself. *Then* we can get the police. I'll go and get Shasta, you get the tack.'

'No we won't, we'll both go and get both,' Chris said firmly. 'Anyway, I wouldn't know what to bring.'

How thankful I was to have Chris with me! All the horror of my encounter with Mr Betts came vividly back to me. If I hadn't been afraid for Shasta I couldn't have gone on.

We left our bikes in the lane and looked cautiously into the yard. The Landrover and a trailer were parked there, blocking our view of Shasta's box. No one was about.

'They could be in the tack-room or the office,' I said in a whisper.

'Or in the pony-field,' Chris said more optimistically.

We stood for a few moments by the gateway. The trailer — an old one, not much used nowadays — had its ramp down. For Shasta?

'They could be in her box,' I whispered through stiff, dry lips.

'They wouldn't be so stupid.'

Chris walked boldly into the yard. I hurried after him towards Shasta's box, hoping there was no one to see.

'Take it calmly. Be normal,' Chris said in a low voice.

'They'll tear me limb from limb!'

We walked across the yard and round the trailer. She must have heard us coming, for Shasta's lovely head appeared at her door.

'Oh Chris, she's still here!' I ran forward and hugged her hard grey neck. The relief was unbelievable. Behind me Chris, who was looking into the back of the trailer, said, 'There's a saddle and stuff in here. You don't think they're Shasta's, do you?'

I released Shasta and joined him. In the shadows at the far end of the trailer hung a saddle and bridle.

I went in to look at it, followed by Chris. And then everything happened at once. We were hurled violently forward from behind, pitched stumblingly on top of one another. Bolts were shot home. There was darkness.

Then, as we picked ourselves up, we heard the sound of the Landrover's engine. The trailer jerked forward. We were prisoners.

13

The great day of the show

IT WAS PITCH DARK inside the trailer. We were driven for perhaps ten or fifteen minutes, the last part over rough ground, moving slowly. Then we stopped. The engine was switched off. Sudden silence.

'Let us out! Let us out!' we yelled, thumping on the walls.

No one came. The silence was complete, the trailer in darkness.

Chris said, 'I always thought the back of these things was open at the top.'

'So is this one if you leave the top doors open,' I answered. But it was no good – both upper and lower door sections were now securely fastened. I rattled and banged them in frustration.

'Not even a window,' said Chris.

I abandoned my assault on the doors. 'I've an idea there ought to be a window at the front,' I said.

'Is it big enough to get out of?' Chris felt around on the front wall for the window-frame.

'Not a hope. It was just a sort of peephole. The glass got broken and Rob boarded it up,' I said, remembering.

In the darkness Chris had found the window-frame. 'I'm going to smash it open. It feels like plywood or something.'

'You can't do it with your hands.'

'I wasn't going to.'

I heard Chris fumbling about on the trailer floor, then there were blows and a splintering sound higher up at the window. A small jagged area of light appeared. Chris put his face to it and looked out.

'We're in a wood. Quite well in, I'd say. That's why it looks so dark.' He moved his head from the hole and looked at his watch. 'Nine o'clock. Looks as though we could be here for the night.'

'Oh, don't say that! What about Shasta? What about the show? Let's make a noise. There might be somebody about, walking a dog or something.'

We shouted and banged until our fists were sore and our throats aching. The old Hollin Bank trailer, which Mr Bryant jokingly told pupils had been used to ferry animals to the ark, stood up well to our efforts.

When it was dark outside and no one had come we resigned ourselves to sleeping on the floor. We sat on the hard rubber matting with out backs against the wall and I filled Chris in on the day's events. Gradually the dim square of window, no bigger than my head, merged into the darkness of the walls. I thought of Dad back at home. Surely he would come to look for us? But Dad, late in, would probably assume we were in bed already. He would go quietly upstairs to avoid waking us. He wouldn't even expect to see me at breakfast because I had planned to leave so early.

'What time do you get up on Saturdays?' I asked Chris.

'Dad and I were going to leave for the show at nine.'

Breakfast about eight then, I thought. At what time would Dad realize that Chris wasn't there?

I imagined him calling upstairs, getting more and more impatient, then going up and finding the empty rooms. What time would that be? Twenty past eight? Half past? Certainly too late for me to ride at Hensingham.

'They're going to keep us here until after the show,' I thought numbly. 'They're keeping Shasta from the show to teach me a lesson.' After the show Chris and I would be released with a great display of astonishment and the pretence that we had been shut in by mistake. But Shasta's chance in the Foxhunter would be gone.

The long night wore on. By morning any stolen horses would be gone. All evidence removed. All tracks covered. The police would find nothing wrong.

And Shasta? 'Oh God, please keep Shasta safe!' I prayed desperately. 'Please let her still be there!' I kept saying it in my mind for what seemed like hours. 'If we are part of God's family,' Mum used to say, 'our problems are his problems.' All we had to do was to trust him, and to thank him for his goodness that wanted the best for us even more than we wanted it ourselves. 'Oh *please* take care of Shasta,' I whispered. 'Please make it all come right!'

At long, long last, after what seemed like half a lifetime, a faint grey light showed at the window. And after that I think I must have slept, for when I looked again the light was paler and the slumped shape of Chris was discernible, asleep on the floor. Hensingham Show! As the light grew stronger I thought of Hollin Bank. Soon the horses would be whinnying and banging their doors wanting breakfast. The Bryants and Mr Betts would arrive, making an early start on the day's work before leaving for the show. Rob's transistor would be on as he got Coppernob ready.

Would he wonder what had happened to *me*? I wondered. Would he wonder why I wasn't up there with Shasta? Or did Rob know why already?

The light at the window grew stronger. In the wood outside the birds were awake. Sunlight touched the leaves. Six o'clock came. Seven. If only we could get out! I thumped despairingly on the thin walls.

The thumping woke Chris, who rolled over and groaned. At the same time — unbelievably — I heard footsteps in the wood!

'Chris, wake up! There's someone coming!'

Chris was awake at once and getting to his feet. Weariness vanished. 'Help!' we yelled at the tops of our voices. 'Let us out!'

Now the footsteps were right alongside. At any moment the bolts would be drawn back, the daylight flood in. I might even have time to get to the show.

We heard a door being opened. But it was the Landrover's door, not ours. The engine started up. We were jerked forward. We weren't being released after all. We were simply being moved elsewhere!

I peered out of the little window. All I could see was the back of the Landrover, leaves overhead. The ground was so bumpy I was almost jolted off my feet. Then there was a smoother section — road? — and then a bumpy stretch again. We swung right then left. In the silence after the engine was switched off we heard the sharp whinny of a horse and felt the trailer being unhitched. Then the Landrover was driven away.

Chris looked out of the window. 'I can see buildings,' he said.

I didn't need to look. The bumpy lane and the sounds of the place were unmistakable. 'We're back at Hollin Bank,' I said. 'They've brought us back!'

'I don't see why you're so excited about it,' Chris said gloomily. 'I thought you said there'd be no one here today. That's probably why they brought us. In the wood we might have been heard.'

'Be quiet a minute. I'm sure I heard Shasta just then!' I listened but the whinny I had heard was not repeated. All the same, I was sure it was Shasta. Oh, if only we could get out!'

'Let us out! Let us out!' I shouted, thumping the walls again.

'I'm starving,' said Chris. 'And thirsty. If we're going to be here all day I hope they'll bring us some food.'

'But then they couldn't pretend it was a mistake!'

I reasoned that our jailer must be Mr Betts, for all the others would have already left for the show. Copper and Fandango, groomed and resplendent and wearing their new blue travelling bandages, would be travelling in the horse-box with Mrs Bryant's Bay Robin. I pictured the scene at Hensingham. Horse-boxes, lorries, cattle-trucks and cars would be converging on the show-field from every direction. Flags would be flying bravely over the white tents, Women's Institute ladies would be putting up their displays of patchwork and home-grown vegetables. Officials would be testing loudspeakers.

I should have been a part of it. And now it was too late.

And then, quite unexpectedly, when we had given up all hope, we heard voices. A woman's voice and a girl's. There was the sound of a horse being led across the yard.

'It's Susi Hollyhock!' I shouted, wild with delight. 'Susi! Let us out of here!'

I had completely forgotten that Susi was going to the show. Her class was later than ours. In the past week, with the ET's and everything, I had scarcely seen her.

Now we heard her quick footsteps and the drawing back of the bolts. When she dropped down the ramp and found me and Chris her face was the picture of astonishment.

It was wonderful to be free again and out in the sunshine. Susi's parents were there with their car and trailer. Her mother, dressed for work, hair tied back with a scarf, was coming out of Hollyhock's box with a bucket.

'I thought you had entered the Foxhunter,' Susi

said. 'I thought you were leaving early. Shasta's been going mad.'

Leaving Chris to make some sort of explanation, I raced across to Shasta's box. There she was, the darling lovely creature, looking proudly over her door, her ears alert, her whole being seeming to say, 'When do we go?'

'Oh Shasta!' I flung my arms around her. Tears of happiness flowed down my face. Though the sensible, rational part of me had thought it most unlikely for Shasta to be moved or harmed, because that would have made the Bryants' guilt obvious, the relief of finding that she was safe was incredible. At that moment I didn't care a fig about the show, or about any other show. I didn't even care if it was proved she wasn't mine. I was just full of thankfulness that she was safe.

Chris came up behind me with my grooming-kit. 'Well, jump to it!' he said briskly. 'I thought you said you had a lot to do. Let's get busy.'

Almost automatically I started work. After the strain, the excitement, the relief, my brain was almost numb.

'But I can't understand how it *happened*,' Susi kept saying. 'Why did the Bryants not hear? You can't have been there all *night*!'

'It was a mistake,' I said, brushing Shasta's hard grey flanks. 'I'll tell you when there's more time.'

She brought us food from their car. Chris got drinks from the machine. Everyone was full of sympathy. I plaited Shasta's mane. Susi did her tail and put an extra hay-net and bucket in their trailer for Shasta to use at the show.

When it was time for them to go she came across to me, looking troubled. 'I only wish we had room for you and Shasta as well,' she said. Her pale hair was smooth and shining. She wore immaculate riding clothes, everything neat as a pin. It was how I had hoped to look myself.

'I'm sorry about the Foxhunter.' Her grey eyes – so like Wendy's, though I had never noticed it until today – looked at me sympathetically.

'It can't be helped.' I watched Hollyhock walk sedately up the ramp into their one-horse trailer. Susi and her parents got into the car. They moved slowly off out of the yard, Susi turning to wave and call, 'Good luck!'

Good luck! Left alone in the yard (for Chris had gone down home to collect my clothes and was not yet back) I straightened my aching limbs and gulped back the tears. Good luck! Until Susi had mentioned the Foxhunter I had managed, by blotting out facts, to pretend to myself that somehow I would be there, that by some miracle everything would still be all right. Now, alone and weary, I could avoid the truth no longer. It was half past nine. The Foxhunter started at half past ten. I was tired, dirty and hungry and not yet changed. I had seven miles to hack to the show.

In other words it was hopeless.

'Oh Shasta!' I whispered. I leaned against her neck and sobbed, while she turned her head and gently whickered, trying to nuzzle me. 'Shasta, I'm so sorry,' I gulped. 'It's all gone wrong. This should have been your chance.'

My own chance too. Perhaps the only one we would ever have now of competing together. If Shasta had been stolen I would know by tonight. Tomorrow she might no longer be mine. Black despair swept through me.

Chris zoomed into the yard in Doris. He leaped out and thrust my boots and a pile of clothes into my hands. 'I think I've got everything. It was all hanging up where you said. Come on. Buck up. If you don't get moving you'll never make it!'

I hadn't the heart to say it was too late already. Besides, I didn't trust myself to speak. I brushed the

118

tears from my face then took my things from him, hoping he wouldn't notice anything wrong.

'Dad was mad as anything when I told him we'd been locked in. He phoned the Bryants right away but there was no one there. Anything else I can do to help?'

I shook my head.

'Right, I'll be off, then. See you at the show!'

He zoomed off again, no doubt thinking of breakfast and a shave and a bath with lots of hot water.

I washed my face at the office tap and changed my clothes. In the little mirror my face looked blotched and haggard and red-eyed. By now the other Foxhunter entrants would be riding smartly round the field, greeting one another speculating about the course. Utter hopelessness gripped me. 'Oh, Heavenly Father, please help me!' I heard myself saying through my tears.

I don't know what sort of help I expected it to be, but there was certainly nothing I could do to help myself. I was too late and that was that. As I came out of the office the words 'God is faithful' and the happy scene on my poster came into my mind. Then I saw Shasta standing at the far side of the yard, tossing her head under a cobalt sky, and felt a sudden rush of affection and pride. After all, Shasta herself was an answer to prayer. I might never have had her at all! I had asked for a horse and God had given me Shasta. Surely I could continue to trust him now? Instead, all I had been doing was to feel sorry for myself because I couldn't ride in a particular competition. It was a very humbling thought.

'Come along, Shasta, we're going to the show,' I said as I tacked her up. Shasta was impatient to be off.

It was useless, I knew, but it was better than doing nothing. And sometimes miracles did happen, I reminded myself. Perhaps the class would be very late starting?

Going up the lane from the stables Shasta would have trotted but I held her back. Time enough for trotting when she had warmed up. What was trotting speed – seven miles an hour? Eight? Perhaps there would be stretches where we could canter.

Seven miles to the show. Fifty minutes until the class was due to start. As Shasta's eager stride carried me forward between the hedgerows I hardly dared to look at my watch. We went past our house and the Bonds' at a fast trot. Could I really expect Shasta to jump after travelling there at such a pace, I wondered?

When we joined the main road we came upon a string of traffic crawling towards Hensingham, though the far side of the road was almost empty. We trotted along on the wide verge, passing the cars. Five miles and thirty-five minutes to go. And that was without checking in or getting my number.

It was impossible! If I looked at the position fair and square I would have to admit it. Even if we did get there in time Shasta would be in no condition to go straight into a big class. What was the point in rushing like this – for nothing? 'If you are just going for the sake of a day out, why not go home first and get properly tidied up?' said the discouraging voice inside me.

Shutting such thoughts firmly from my mind, I watched the traffic go past – more quickly now because there was a clearer spell – and wondered what Dad and Chris were doing. They would have arrived there ages ago, looking for me in the crowds. 'And you won't be there in time,' said the voice of self-pity. 'However hard you try.'

But to be beaten, in the end, by such a small margin! With half an hour more I could have done it. Less if the class was late. Tears of frustration pricked my eyes.

I was jerked out of my gloom by a loud tooting from behind. Instinctively I drew Shasta nearer the hedge. The tooting persisted. 'Idiots!' I thought, leaning forward to calm her. Glancing over my shoulder I saw a trailer right up on the verge where it widened by a gate. Someone was shouting my name.

I reined in and looked back. Susi was pelting along the grass towards us.

'Quick, let's get Shasta loaded,' she gasped, catching hold of the reins. 'We'll have you there in no time!'

14

. . . and how it all ended

AFTER THAT, everything went like a dream. With six hands to help, Shasta was bandaged and loaded and we were on our way almost before I had grasped what was happening.

Susi had left Hollyhock with her mother as soon as they had reached the showground and had come back at once to fetch us. 'It'll be touch and go as regards time,' she said, 'but they're always a little bit late. If you go and check in we'll see to Shasta and bring her to the collecting ring.'

It was unbelievable. Fifteen minutes earlier I had been riding desperately along the verge. Now here I was at the showground going to collect my number.

Susi stood by the rail with Shasta while I walked the course. Luckily, as she had supposed, the class was late.

Inspecting the gate, I was startled to find myself next to Rob, who was doing the same. Was I mistaken or was Rob also surprised to see *me*? 'Thought you'd got lost or something,' he said and strode off with Sue Kettlewell.

The course was much as Wendy had predicted. At least I had had no time to be nervous. I rode in for my round quite calmly, and I had the most extraordinary feeling that now I had safely arrived everything else would drop into place too. It was a clear round! I rode out of the ring on a tide of happiness. But it wasn't just the clear round. It was the sort of deep-down happy feeling that comes from knowing God had heard my prayer and answered it. Of knowing that he cared about me.

Susi was waiting to go in on Hollyhock. 'Oh, that was splendid,' she said, her eyes shining. 'Rob always said you should push her more. I expect that now he's wishing he'd never mentioned it!'

'*Did* I push her?'

'You sort of rode more positively. It obviously pays off. Wish me luck! I've got butterflies big as turkeys batting about inside me.'

I had never seen Susi compete before. She rode with a lot of dash and style, not at all in the calm way I had expected. She knocked down the gate, a brick from the wall and a plank. The brick was unlucky, because Hollyhock barely tipped it. They cantered back into the collecting ring with a flourish.

'Oh well, the end of a perfect mess,' she said as she slipped from the saddle. 'Let's get an ice-cream or something. They'll be ages before your jump-off. We can eat them while we watch.'

We tied the horses to the railings, where Susi's mother put on their fly sheets and gave them sugar. The queue at the ice-cream van was still a mile long so we went to the nearby refreshment tent for cans of drinks instead.

'Tepid,' said Susi in disgust as we walked back to the ring. 'We've got cold drinks in the car but it's so far back to the car park. Mum keeps them in the freezer-bag. Will you be able to have lunch with us?'

My heart skipped a beat. Lunch from the back of the car with Susi and her family – I would be a part of the great friendly crowd, just like everyone else.

'I expect Dad will have brought something,' I said reluctantly. I didn't even know where he was parked.

'Oh well, there'll be other times,' she said. 'Look, isn't that Rob's head bobbing around the ring? Let's see how he's getting on. I expect Mr and Mrs Bryant will be somewhere about.'

A meeting with the Bryants was what I had been dreading. Luckily for me, when we reached the rails we saw them some distance away. They didn't appear to notice us and afterwards moved off into the crowd. Nor did I meet them in the car park. I exchanged brief words with Rob during classes and glimpsed Mrs Bryant on Bay Robin, but that was all.

The meeting would have to come, but I was glad it didn't spoil that happy, exhausting, glorious day. Looking back on it I remember blue skies, smiling faces, hooves thudding over green grass; Chris, Dad and I enjoying our picnic lunch; Susi in her showing class while I sat and watched and ate chocolate with her parents; Wendy's suntanned face as she chatted to me in the collecting ring; and Sherry and her family, clutching large ice-creams, clustering importantly round Shasta like self-appointed guardian angels.

Oh – and, amazingly, in the Foxhunter I was placed second. Rob and Fandango came sixth.

When, tired and contented, Shasta and I returned to Hollin Bank that evening there was a police car parked outside the bungalow.

The sight of it brought me back to earth with a bump. I went on down to the stables with a feeling of dread to bed Shasta down for the night. Rob and his mother were busy catching up on the evening stablework. As we worked we exchanged brief comments about the show. No one mentioned the police car. I was sure it must have come because of Dad's phone call.

Susi and Hollyhock were not yet back. I had left the show early, having work to do. How I wished they were there! Or Mrs Gale. Even the presence of a few pupils would have given an air of normality and lessened the tension.

It was not until the next day that I learned what had happened. Most surprisingly I had the news from Sherry. The Bonds had left the show even before I had because of Mr Bond having to dismantle Tychwell's market stalls, and Sherry, at a loose end, had taken Chris's bike and gone up to Hollin Bank in search of action.

There she had discovered the police van, and seen (presumably by peeping through the windows) Mr Betts being questioned by an Inspector. By the time she arrived at the stables next morning she had the full story.

The police, she said, were investigating the theft of the dyed pony, which Mr Betts had been hiding at Hollin Bank on behalf of a friend. The two of them had been dealing in stolen ponies for some months, and the police were very glad to have caught up with them at last. Most of the stolen ponies had at some time been kept in the disused, isolated cottage up in the wood, near where I had found the hoofprints when looking for Lara.

Mr Bryant was completely innocent. He had known nothing of this at all, not even about the dyed freeze-brand. Mr Betts had told him that the pony must be kept isolated in case it was developing influenza, so when he heard the truth he was quite shattered. That morning as he fed and mucked out he worked in silence, instead of his usual cheerful singing. From time to time he shook his head in disbelief, muttering things under his breath.

I also learned something else during the next few days. It was such a relief to find that Mr Bryant's brusque manner to me in the days before the show had not been due to a guilty conscience or the suspicion that I was snooping on him, but because Mr Betts had led him to believe that I had been taking extra feed for Shasta. In fact, it had been taken by Mr Betts himself to feed the stolen pony in the cottage.

There was still one thing that bothered me. I knew that sometime I would have to clear it up, and I racked my brain for days for a tactful way of doing it. At last I decided I would simply have to go ahead and ask.

I found Mr Bryant alone in the office, searching the desk, and took my courage in both hands. Before I could change my mind I said, 'Mr Bryant, I would like to ask you something.'

He looked up at me kindly and paused.

'It's about Shasta. Mr Betts told me she had been stolen.'

For an instant he gazed at me in astonishment. Then his face creased up in laughter. 'My word, that's a good one!' he said. 'If anyone was robbed it was me! Do you know how much I lost on that sale, young lady?' He turned back to the desk drawer. 'I've probably still got the receipt somewhere. I knew how much you wanted her, and how much your Dad would pay, so I had to pretend I didn't know a lot about her or otherwise you'd have thought I needed my head examining. Just do well with her, that's all I ask. Rob's always wanting me to buy her back, but I don't think there'll be much chance of that after your performance at Hensingham.'

It took me a moment or two to work out what he was saying. 'Oh Mr Bryant, thank you!' I stammered. 'I don't know what to say.'

Mr Bryant hated anything emotional. He was essentially a very practical sort of man. 'Just look at the mess in these drawers,' he said, quickly changing the subject. 'One of these days I must get round to sorting it. I once had a first-class rocket from the bank – real "pay up or else" stuff – when all the time there were two envelopes here stuffed with cheques, just waiting to be taken in. Paperwork isn't my strong point, I'm afraid.'

So the last of the mysteries was solved and Shasta was truly mine. The week sped by. Soon there'd be another bunch of ET's arriving.

On the Friday Wendy came into the tack-room to say goodbye before leaving for her holiday in France. I'd miss her a lot while she was away.

'Well, at least we've got someone to help with the stablework for the holidays,' Rob said when she had gone. 'With uncle gone *and* Wendy away we would have been in a real fix. She's starting tomorrow. Seemed quite pleased to be asked, in fact.'

'*Who*?'

'Why, Susi of course,' said Rob. 'Didn't Dad tell you?'

Susi Hollyhock working at the stables. I couldn't imagine anything better! Susi, who had been such a good friend at the show. Susi, who had asked me to have lunch with them and said, 'There'll be other times.' And to think she was actually coming to work with me!

I must have been standing there in amazement for some time. Then I realized Rob was looking at me curiously. 'What's the matter?' he asked. 'I thought you two were friends.'

Suddenly I was bursting with happiness. 'Yes,' I said, remembering the poster. 'Yes. I think we shall be!'